Halfway to the Stars

Halfway to the Stars

Cable Car Tales of a Grumpy Gripman

by

Daniel Curzon

Daniel Curzon

Halfway to the Stars – Cable Car Tales of a Grumpy Gripman

Published by l'Aleph – Sweden
www.l-aleph.com

ISBN 978-91-7637-574-7

l'Aleph is a Wisehouse Imprint.

© Wisehouse 2014 – Sweden
www.wisehouse-publishing.com

For Chip Palmer,

the late

MUNI driver

(1943- 2003)

This is a work of fiction.

And every word of it is true.

First off, despite what you may have heard, the cable cars don't really climb halfway to the stars. I know you want them to. So do I. Believe me, they go in far more "interesting" directions than just to the stars.

Now this book isn't about me. It's about the people I have encountered, whether I wanted to or not, as a longtime gripman working on San Francisco's cable cars. It has been my job for 25 years (since I was 27) to operate the two-lever "grip" on the three lines of cable cars: the one on Powell / Hyde Streets, plus the Powell / Mason line, and the one up and down California Street. The levers in the front of each cable car (at both ends on the California line) are big and thick and can be murder on the arms, hands and back. You should see my chest and forearms. My legs are strong too, especially the calves. At least that's what my girlfriend, Darlene, tells me. It's just that I need a little more Ibuprofen on a run now than I used to. I'm not complaining. I love my job – most of the time.

Well, "love" may be too strong a word, actually. I know I can't keep going forever, especially having to stand all the time. Whenever a supervisor comes around checking on us, I make sure I don't utter a single groan or show the slightest hesitation in keeping the cable cars doing their thing.

Just between you and me, the supervisor ought to be looking at some of the conductors.

How shall I put it? They pilfer cash, and it happens more than you think. I've seen it with my own eyes. We're not supposed to tattle on one another. But no wonder the cable cars don't pay for themselves! There is even talk of shutting them down permanently because they lose money. Won't happen. The cable cars are too "colorful." What's the phrase for that? Is it LOL? Or maybe LMAO? Boy, is my ass laughing!

On the cable cars to move forward, when the center plate is lowered, the hinges fastened to it are forced by rollers to tighten two dies against the cable, in a vise-like grip. If that isn't fascinating enough, there is also a foot brake, a track brake to slow down even more, and what we call "putting the wood down" to stop. I also have a rope connected to a bell that I use to tell motor cars and pedestrians to get the hell out of my way. The conductor has a bell too, but his is smaller than mine! We're not supposed to ring it all the time. But I like to give it a good whacking just for fun as often as I can. During the bell ringing competitions in the summer, I usually win. A bell to ring and a thermos of hot tea close by and I'm rarin' to roll!

Ready for some charming stories, or maybe some not so charming? If you're game, I'm game. Some people might find me a little prickly or grumpy. Bullshit! No Sacred Cows allowed here.

Let me tell you a little tale about the nun who used to ride my line, not every day, just once in a while. She was a tall, lean, aesthetic-looking person, certainly 6'5," I would guess. She wore the traditional stiff nun headwear – the wimple, I think it's called – and a black and white habit, wore sensible nun shoes, and carried a large pocketbook, in which she kept Kleenex, three rosaries, various sunglasses, old sandwiches, and white eye-liner. (I believe she was a man underneath all the trappings. I was too much of a good Stockton boy to ask!) She kept her eyes downcast like a real lady nun much of the time, except when she jumped up and wolf-whistled at handsome men on different corners as we whisked by on our ride.

One day I noticed that Sister Apassionatta of the Ladder-Day Sinners (the name by which she identified herself) looked somewhat downcast. I try to be friendly, sort of, to all my passengers, to make the time pass as much as anything, and so I asked her what was wrong.

At first she said, "Nothing."

But I sensed that she wanted to say more. "Are you sure?" I asked.

A small tear appeared in one eye, and when she wiped it away she irritated her white eye-liner, and it got into her eye and made her cry even more.

"Is it your love life, Sister?" I said, being a wise-ass.

"No, not that," she replied. "You'd be surprised how many straight married guys want to take me out."

"Really?" I stammered. I pulled on the grip to make the next stop, at Front Street. People jumped on and off as they do, and I had to tell two teenagers not to hang off the side. (They ignored me, of course. I didn't smack them. See how loveable I am!)

When I looked over at the nun, I noticed that she looked like she was going to throw herself from the cable car. "Sister, no!" I yelled.

She looked back at me, annoyed. "I was just throwing up. I wasn't going to jump!" she said with great force. "Not all drag queens are suicidal, asshole!" she added.

"Sorry," I said insincerely. Please! I have never met people more fussy about the differences between Them and Us and explaining it "just so," than your San Francisco "trans" persons! Give me a break. A few years ago most of the passengers would have tossed her "trans" ass under the goddamn cable car, never mind using the correct term while doing it.

Anyhow, I saw her sit down again, not get off at her usual stop. "Do you mind if I stay on a while?" she suddenly asked me. "Until my stomach settles." We don't like passengers to keep riding for hours on the same fare. Call us cheapskates, but there are so many people wanting to ride, mostly tourists, that we have to clear the cars each time to keep traffic flowing. The cars are not even that comfortable, just "picturesque," so I don't know why you'd want to stay on them as long as I have to! I also didn't want her throwing up on the other passengers. "It's also Ladder Day, did you know? Please," she added.

"Sure, stay as long as you want this time, Sister," I said. (What the fuck is Ladder Day?)

"This is my last ride," she answered, looking directly into my eyes.

"Oh, my God, no!" I cried out.

"Yes, I am going to a hospice at the top of the line," she explained.

"Is it AIDS?" I wondered.

"No, a brain tumor."

"Oh, my God."

"Indeed, God is calling me to His bosom, with my very own brain tumor. Needless to say, it's inoperable."

"Did you get a second opinion?"

"Yes, I asked Sister Sherschlock Porot at our convent. In ordinary life she is a surgeon at Kaiser."

"I'm very sorry."

"We all have to go sometime," she said, flinging the back of her hand to her forehead in a rather large gesture. It made me wonder if she was telling the truth. But some people are just "Bigger Than Life," I figure. You got to go with it.

So Sister and I plus the others hopping on and off rode up and down California Street for several hours. She pointed over a few blocks to where she had gone to Catholic school until the eighth grade – and had even been an altar boy. She mentioned a little anecdote about a charming rector at Grace Cathedral, where Sister said she had studied to be a deacon in her twenties, only to drop out when a homophobic Pope was elected. She pointed out an abandoned building where she had performed for the first time in nun's drag, or "habit-forming apparel," as she termed it. She seemed to be re-living those moments from her life, even crossing herself each time we passed one of them.

Finally, we got up to the top of California again, at Van Ness, and Sister seemed about to disembark from the cable car. She lingered for a few seconds as the car lurched to a stop, one white-knuckled hand gripping an overhead strap. "How much do I owe you for all the extra trips today?" she asked. "I guess I should have bought the all-day pass."

"Nothing, Sister. It's on me. It's on the City."

"Why, thank you, sir!" she exclaimed.

"It's the least I can do."

"Would you like my number?"

I hesitated. "Your telephone number?"

"I can always tell," she said.

C3 80

Okay, so I had a couple of dates with a man-nun with a brain tumor! Upon occasion, I'm a little bi. So sue me!

(Besides, I think she lied about the brain tumor. I heard she moved to Atlanta.)

୯ଛ ଧ

Many times I wondered about the homeless woman with one tooth as I rode up and down the cable car routes. Usually she was somewhere on the Powell / Mason Street line, probably because the begging was better there, but from time to time I would see her on Hyde Street. You could tell that she had once been a pretty woman, maybe even a beautiful one. Now time and fortune had taken their toll. Her face was a crazy quilt of lines and scars, her hair old, thin and scraggly, blowing around her head like some Renaissance Venus on acid. Except for the one bottom tooth, which she stuck out far too much, her mouth was tiny and feminine. She never actually rode the cable cars, or mine at least. Instead, she sat on the sidewalk against the sides of different high rise buildings. She wore a head scarf for "modesty," but she also sometimes sat with her skirt hiked up to her thighs, apparently unaware of the discrepancy – or of the cold, foggy San Francisco mornings.

Other riders noticed her as well, and various stories were traded over the years. Some thought she was the illegitimate daughter of some barbarian prince exiled to America for some old-fashioned offense, one that no longer even considered an offense in the States. Some thought she was a Jewish princess from Shaker Heights, Ohio, who had gotten into heavy drugs as a girls' academy and just kept moving west until she had nowhere else to go. Some thought she was twins, or even triplets, and that it wasn't the same person out there on the streets all those times. One old lady from Pacific Heights even thought, the homeless woman was "faking it" and was "richer than God."

One day I saw her being hit on the top of the head by some fat guy with a rolled-up *Chronicle*. Or maybe an *Examiner*, since so many of those were lying around unread all over the place. I even was about to stop the cable car and jump off and stop the fat guy, but he saw me and shook his fist and went into his liquor store. Evidently Miss One-Tooth had urinated on the sidewalk in front of his place of business. Don't get me wrong. I am no bleeding heart when it comes to the "homeless." One followed me once with a tin cup with a single coin inside it, shaking it very hard as he walked behind me. "It could be a gun! It could be a gun!" he kept saying. Fuck him! I could have a gun too, asshole! And there would be fewer creeps like you on the streets of San Francisco!

But the One-Toothed Lady seemed vulnerable and never bothered me, and I didn't want anybody beating on her, for God's sake. What have we come to?!

One time she did start to board my cable car, but she couldn't make it up because the step is so high. I even tried to lift her up, knowing that she probably wouldn't be able to pay, but she pointed to her arm, indicating that I was pinching her. So I let go. "Thank you so very mush," she said in a foreign accent. It might have been South American. I'm terrible at accents. I just went as far as high school. Hers had a Hispanic tinge to it. (They speak Spanish in South America, right? The Conquistadors or somebody like that. It's hard to keep up!)

Anyway, her grey eyes were very soft, despite the scabs and sores and God knows what, all over her forehead, chin and cheeks. She was bundled up in a bulky old faded sweater that had seen better days. She kept staring at me as my cable car moved away up the hill. "Thank God you not let her on!" a sneering old Chinese lady in a seat near me said. "She *stink*!"

"We all stink some time," I muttered.

"*I* never stink!" the old Chinese lady said, holding her four grocery bags on her lap as if I might steal them. I know for a fact that she got the groceries free as a Catholic food bank across town. So why so self-righteous? It was the same old rather large Chinese lady who had gotten into a fist fight with some young ghetto woman with Bad Attitude and had then pushed her off the cable car and flat on her Bad Attitude ass on the tracks. (I was with the old Chinese lady on that one. No White Guilt for her!)

As for One Tooth, I did not see her for some time, probably six months, and then there she was again. I wish I could say that she had gotten her life together and was now working at Twitter for a very high salary. In fact, she looked worse than ever. She didn't even make eye contact with me when I passed by, as she had before. From my perspective she looked dazed and confused. She had lost weight, something she didn't have much of to begin with. She did seem to be with a man, who looked as bad as she did. He wore a tattered old cap and a black overcoat that was too tight on him. He looked about fifty to her thirty – both going on sixty. He wasn't very nice to her, you could tell, although you couldn't make out the exact words. I don't think he was her pimp, just her "boyfriend." "What some people will do to have a boyfriend!" (That's what my girl, Darlene, always says. Yeah, well, fuck her. I don't beat her up!)

I finally learned what had happened to One-Tooth to make her into the sad character she had become. She staggered up to my cable car one afternoon with some newspapers outstretched in her hand. "Kindly read about me," she said. She attempted a smile, but it was not a success. "People saved me!" she said as she moved away, back to her "boyfriend," who evidently was making her give away her few possessions. I never saw her again after that day.

The newspapers were years old, yellowed, and ripped around the edges. When I opened the first one, there was a photograph of the One-Toothed Woman in her prime. Not only did she have all her teeth, they were perfect ones. Her face was flawless and downright regal. In the sub-headline she was even referred to as "Ex-Miss Chile." So she had been an actual beauty queen.

The news story was about how her husband at the time, an elected official of the City and County of San Francisco, had been arrested for grabbing her shoulder during an argument and leaving a small bruise. A neighbor had snapped a photo of the bruise and it had wound up in the police department, where it had become the subject of a "spousal abuse" charge. The beauty queen and the official both claimed that it was a one-time event and that the woman was unusually susceptible to bruising because of her delicate skin.

As I read on through the newspaper accounts, it turned out that the official was convicted, had to give up his position, was reinstated, then removed in a recall election, could not find another job, soon had to sell everything to pay his legal bills, and eventually divorced his wife. The exhausted former husband shot himself a couple of years later. That's when the Beauty Queen was left with no money, no income, caught in an immigration quagmire, and wound up living destitute and abused on the streets of San Francisco. (Yeah, they sure "saved" her alright, those bleeding heart saviors. People get these "ideas" in their heads that defy common sense. You got to watch out for them. They'll force you to believe what they do, despite your own eyes, just like the other side does, those Holier Than Thou religious types. (I can't stand either side.)

&#x3; &#x2;

The California line runs close to Chinatown. It's okay to sat "Chinatown," but God help you if you say "Chinaman." (It makes no sense to me, but people around here are so goddamned fussy about terms.) I don't like Chinatown very much. It's way overcrowded, with too many dirty parts, like garbage cans left out, and the windows aren't cleaned much and have these poor ducks hanging up by their necks as if they have been burned by acetylene torches. Jesus

Christ, who'd want to eat those?! I also don't much care for the way the Chinese treat most animals. They don't seem to have the faintest concern about creatures they are going to eat (turtles, fowls, whatever) and keep them under horrendous conditions. We all have to eat, and I'm hardly a duck hugger, but you don't have to torture the critters first. For God's sake, they're still using parts of tigers and rhinos to get better hard-ons, when those animals are almost extinct! The one thing we don't need more of are hordes of Chinese with hard-ons!

I wonder why everybody is so concerned about the Mexicans getting in "illegally" when the Asians are pouring in to San Francisco without so much as a peep? I'm a "minority" now in my own city. Believe me, I don't care for being a "minority." (Unless you want to give me some of that Affirmative Action!) Yeah, you might say I don't subscribe to all the "poor immigrant" crap. Give me your job because a cousin of my grandfather was in an internment camp for a month during World War II. Yeah, sure. My grandfather worked in a tiny hardware store in Youngstown, Ohio from 8 to 8 for 57 years. And he died almost broke. Nobody gave him a damn thing! He gave me a wrench on my fifteenth birthday and said "Keep it. You never know when you might need a wrench." I still keep that wrench in my toolbox. (I may still need it to throw it at some of my unruly passengers!)

So I was not exactly "friends" with this little Chinese guy who rode the California line. I barely nodded at him. And the few times he asked me something I couldn't understand a word he said. Cantonese is, let's face it, a hard, ugly language, and he seemed in no hurry to learn English. At least I learned "*Gung ho, fat choy!*" for Chinese New Year! He was small and frail, although I guess you can't say that about Asians anymore either! (Okay, okay, some of them are much bigger now. It must be the McDonald's!) His lips looked raw and his teeth grimy. He didn't smile much, maybe because of his ugly teeth, maybe because he wasn't too happy. But day after day he rode my cable car. I saw him get off and go into a run-down restaurant, which had partially drawn blinds, and was called the Happy Fish, or something. The happy fish, my ass! Sometimes I could see the staff grabbing fish from the tanks near the door and killing them with several knives and serving them up before you could blink. I think the little frail guy was the dish-washer. What a job! Dish after dish after dish, for years and years and years! I read somewhere that if you set your mind right you can endure anything: "Oh, this dirty plate has a booger on it. How exciting!" "And look, this plate has some spit-out broccoli on the right-hand side!" "And, wowie, this pan has some egg foo yung stuck on like I've never seen before in my entire life!" At least the little guy's hands were clean.

I didn't eat on my cable car that much, and rarely Chinese food, since I don't care for it, to be honest. But sometimes I was in a hurry and so I'd gobble down a salami sandwich or some curry. I do like chicken curry a lot. The day the little guy and I "interacted" was the day my conductor on that day was acting weird – on Seconal, I think. I was trying to get back on schedule and so I scarfed down several bites of chicken curry. The shop advertised it as "Curry in a Hurry." Well, yeah, but if you hurry too much you can "Choke in a Hurry." And that is what I did. Talk about going down the wrong pipe. It wouldn't even go down, whatever pipe it was! I couldn't speak. I couldn't remember the so-called "international signal" for choking: you know, crossed hands at your own throat. My eyes were watering, and I was just about to keel over on the floor of my car and probably die a horrible death without being able to utter a single cry for help. When you're dying, you at least want to be able to call out, for Christ's sake!

When suddenly the little Chinaman (gentleman from China) jumped up from his seat, which was facing out, came around and starting banging on my back. He even forced me to hold my hands over my head. Then he banged me some more. I thought it was useless, but then the chunk of chicken curry flew out of my mouth and landed on a tourist (from Belgium – I remember because he sued and lost.) Now I could breathe again with a bunch of spitting and coughing thrown in. The little guy even gave me a drink of water from a thermos bottle he carried. I have to admit that he probably saved my life that day. The fucked-up conductor certainly didn't!

I still see that little guy every day and he smiles at me. Sometimes he gives me the "international signal" for choking, and I acknowledge my debt to him with a quick nod. He seems to think he owns me now. Yeah, yeah, he was great on that day, and now I can't even hate the Chinese anymore. Damn!

ᑳ ᑰ

There was a boy about nine or ten years old who rode the California line. He stood out because no adults ever seemed to be with him, never. He had black hair and odd little features and wore a really old-fashioned cap with ear flaps. I think he was of "Mixed Race" as we say now. Which races I couldn't tell you. I suppose I'm a "racist," but to be honest I pretty much hate all races equally, depending on the day's events. You don't always see the fucking Public at its best in my line of work. I don't think the conductor made this kid pay his fare. He didn't seem thankful, or even to know that a smile is worth a thousand words. Hell, maybe he had something wrong with his cheek muscles, I don't know! Whatever it was, he hadn't learned how to win a grown-up's heart with a little eye contact, with the BIG EYES, if you get the picture. It didn't even have to be sincere. I would've settled for fake. Still, I felt something for the kid, maybe because I was not a very out-going child myself. I thought everybody was pretty phony and said things they thought would get them ahead, not what they actually felt. I didn't like that at all. In fact, I took a kind of pride in being ornery. This kid I'm talking about wasn't ornery exactly, just emotionless, as cold-hearted as a cat. He never asked me for anything, never spoke to anyone. I sort of wondered why he wasn't in school since he would be on my car during the day. If I had to follow up on every single person who did something wrong on the cable cars, I'd never have time to drive them!

One day I happened to look over and saw the little kid trying to push an old lady carrying a big pocketbook off the cable car. She was waiting for her stop that was coming up. Despite my warning, she had gotten up and waddled to the place where you exit. The car had not stopped yet and was moving along at maybe twelve miles per hour. And this little kid absolutely kept pushing at the old lady until she finally fell off, and before we had come to a complete stop.

Her leg went underneath a back wheel and was run over. It was pretty crushed, but not pretty, let me tell you. I jumped off to see what I could do. The old lady had gone into shock and was out of it. The passengers were all fretting and carrying on, except for the little boy with the ear flaps, who jumped down to the street and looked hard at the woman, with nothing on his face except satisfaction. "Hey, I saw you do that!" I yelled at him. He said nothing. "I'm gonna report you to MUNI!" I added. The little boy just folded his arms over his chest and smirked at me. "You little shit! What the hell's the matter with you?!" I yelled.

"Someone did it to me," he finally answered. "In 1909."

"What?!"

"She's not the first I done it back to," he spat at me. "Or the last."

"You must be nuts," I spat back at him.

"You'd better watch yourself or I might do it to you," the kid said as he started walking away from the cable car.

"Come back here, you!" I called after him. "You won't get away with this!"

Jerry, my conductor that day, Fat Jerry, came up to me to get me to help with the comatose old lady with the crushed leg. "Who are you talking to?" he kind of whispered to me. "The riders are asking if you've gone off the deep end."

"That kid with the ear flaps that's walking away – that's who I'm talking to."

Jerry gave me a funny look and put his finger to his lips to try to get me to shut up.

"Why doesn't somebody stop that kid!" I said to the passengers, pointing hard.

"What are you talking about?" Jerry said, looking both irritated and concerned about me.

"The goddamned kid with the cap with the ear flaps! He pushed the old lady off!"

Everybody looked in the direction I was pointing as the kid fingered his nose at me.

"There's no kid there," Jerry explained. "There's nobody there!"

And when I looked back there was nobody there anymore. I'm sorry. He was there before! He was! I don't believe in any fucking little boy ghosts on the cable cars! He was there!

He was!

CS SO

Clarice and Clementine Jones were twin sisters from the Midwest who had moved to San Francisco years and years ago. They had never married, lived together in North Beach, were not incestuous lesbians, to the best of my knowledge, and had through sheer longevity evolved into a kind of walking tourist attraction. Since they dressed completely alike in tailored red suits, wearing bright red lipstick, too much rouge, and quaint hats from a bygone day, they were sort of delightful. All they had to do was wave now and again, sit on a dais during parades, and let people read into them whatever they wanted. Unlike Emperor Norton in the nineteenth century, the twin sisters were not crazy, just a little eccentric, in a kind of non-threatening British way.

Eventually, though, time caught up with them when they were eighty-four. Their faces got very wrinkled, and Clementine got dementia and kidney disease. She had to go to a care facility. The other one,

Clarice, was lonely because she couldn't see her sister but once a week, if that. They'd had every meal together for over eighty years, usually sausage pizza and orange sherbet, lately in a restaurant near their apartment, but now they were separated from each other.

They had ridden on my cable cars from time to time but came into my life more directly when Clarice went to visit Clementine at the hospital. Alone on the cable car, she wasn't recognized, so I thought I would chat her up. I even offered to buy her lunch.

Here is how it went:

Clarice liked to place her napkin, only cloth of course, at her neck. She may have been trying to disguise the turkey neck, but perhaps she had always preferred it there to on her lap. I think she was developing cataracts in her eyes, which had a certain glassy, thick quality to them. They may have been blue at one time. She did have her very red lipstick on, with a little accidentally smeared on a front tooth.

"Thank you so kindly for taking me to lunch," Clarice said.

"My pleasure," I said.

"Do you have to be back on the cable car soon?"

"I've got a couple of hours."

"I miss Clementine so very much. Sometimes I don't know what to do."

"I'm sorry. It must be difficult."

Clarice sighed.

"Haven't people been kind to you since that article appeared in the paper?"

"Oh, they have. Many, many."

"Well, how great! I wish people would take me out to lunch!" I joked.

"Shall I tell them you want to go?" Clarice asked.

"I was joking," I said. "To look on the positive side, at least now you get to chat with people other than your sister. Diversity and all that."

"Oh, but Filipinos so often want me to go out with them!" she said, with undisguised disdain.

"Oh, you don't care for Filipino food?"

"No, I can't stand the way Filipinos look!" she said. She did not glance around to see if others might overhear her politically incorrect words, as so many of us in the new San Francisco are wont to do.

"At least they try to feed you," I attempted. "I believe they are quite nice to the elderly."

"But who wants to sit opposite Filipinos?! My God, especially the men. They look like turtles! Those pushed-in noses, those scrawny little bodies!" I thought Clarice was going to throw up her sausage pizza.

"Well, I guess there are different tastes," I stammered.

"Why have they let so many of them in – that's what I wonder. I'd much rather look at a Mexican than a Filipino. Wouldn't you?"

I really didn't know what to say.

Clarice helped me out. "Not that I want to look at Mexicans either! Some of the Spanish ones aren't too bad, but those with the Indian blood – oh, my God, so unfortunate! And they'll murder you if you're wear the wrong color! And my sister and I always wear red!"

"I think that may be just for certain gang members," I said.

"Oh, no, it's most of them. Have you been to the courts at 850 Bryant Street? Clementine and I had to go there for some event. My Heavens, the place was crawling with Mexicans. Pardon me, I mean Hispanics. They were also from places like Nicaragua, Panama, and such. Or is it *Latinos*? I can never remember." Well, Clarice had the proper Spanish pronunciation of Latinos politically correct at least!

"How's the pizza?" I asked.

"It's lovely. Thank you again."

"You're welcome."

"The other group at the courts were blacks, just tons of them."

"How about Asians?" I asked.

"Just a few of those. But blacks and Latinos everywhere! Most of them surly and slouchy and just horrible. We sat there and listened for several hours about all the crimes they were accused of. And it wasn't just marijuana. It was beating their girlfriends and whipping their children and robbing old ladies in shopping malls, and shootings and stabbings and putting on dog fights. You name it, they did it. I know they were considered innocent until proven guilty, but my word!"

"Well, maybe the police singled them out, profiled them."

"You think so?" Clarice replied. "I suspect they caught only a small part of the problem. It just keeps getting worse and worse! Clementine and I were finding it harder and harder to go for our walk without being harassed in some way. It's become some sort of horrible Third World country around here. Maybe it's a good thing she has gotten sick."

"I'm sorry to hear it."

"And everywhere blacks become the majority, the places become unlivable. Look at Detroit, Chicago, Oakland, New Orleans, Newark, Johannesburg..." Clarice paused, as if expecting me to supply more cities. When I didn't, she added: "It's not about little Negro girls in yellow dresses trying to go to school anymore, let me tell you! They got into the school, and now they're on crack and vandalizing the place!"

"Are you ready for your sherbet yet?" I enquired.

"In a few minutes. Do you want to leave? I'm enjoying our conversation immensely. It's almost as if you have taken Clementine's place."

"Oh, I'm sure I could never take her place," said I. (Well, maybe on some days!)

"I guess immigrants do a lot of domestic work these days. And my sister and I see – saw a lot of them working in restaurants."

"I hear they do a lot of the jobs Americans don't want to do."

"Even more, they want to commit the crimes Americans don't want to commit!" said Clarice. "I much preferred the old San Francisco, before we had all this god-awful diversity! When it was charming and nice and clean!" She finished off her second slice of pizza with relish.

"Well, it's been very interesting having lunch with you," I said, signaling the server.

"Don't get me started on the gays!" she said.

"Are they having dog fight too?"

"Not that so much. They flaunt it, though."

"Flaunt what?"

"They kiss each other in public now! They dress up."

"I guess it could be looked at as native customs, sort of like an ethnic parade in Bulgaria or somewhere."

"I guess you don't mind it, but Clementine and I just hated to have to sit next to those awful drag queens! Some of them even dressed up in red suits like us!"

"How frightening," I said.

"I guess you don't agree with me," Clarice said, throwing her napkin onto the table. "But isn't all too true. Isn't it? Am I making it up?"

"Maybe we had better discuss the weather," I answered.

"I actually hate San Francisco's weather," she said. "It's so damned cold all the time! Back home, we had some heat!"

"Do you ever go back to visit?" I said slyly.

"Can't afford to. We moved out here and made our bed. Now we can never go back."

"What will you do if your sister passes?"

"I'll be devastated. That's why I've agree to donate a kidney to her."

"You're a match, I take it."

"We are. The trouble is I only have one kidney. We both only have one kidney each."

I took that in. "Then that means . . . that you . . ."

"Will be dead in a few months."

"Oh, my God!"

"But it also means that Clementine and I will have that final time together, and she will probably outlast me by several years."

"But then she will be alone?"

"She will be. But perhaps you can take her out to lunch? You've been so generous and nice. I think you'd like her. She's very much like me."

"Let me ponder that," I said.

And Clarice did sacrifice herself for Clementine, because she was family.

But I never had lunch with her again. Because she was too liberal for me! (That's a joke!) No, I was too afraid to be seen with them and possibly overheard by the P.C. Thought Police.

ꜿ ꜩ

My girlfriend, Darlene, rode on my car today. She is hardly a girl, and sometimes I think she's not much of a friend, but we've been a "couple" for at least five years now, even though we have separate places. She is older than me, by at least 6 years. So that makes her 58. She still looks good, though she's filling in, as they say. She has black hair. She won't tell me if she dyes it, but I think she does. It's sort of stiff. She says it's from her "gypsy blood." Her eyes are a kind of cloudy brown, and she wears too much perfume. She also has this metal rod that she sticks in the side of her nose sometimes. I hate it. We argue about it. She says I should lose twenty pounds, which is irrelevant to her nose piercing. She is working on her Master's in Sustainability, whatever the Hell that is. She also does freelance editing for doctoral theses and stuff like that. (More than she's supposed to, I think.) She's always tired, overworked, always seems a bit groggy. We haven't had sex for about a year now. Maybe it's over. I still like Darlene, but sometimes you just have to move on. I think I'll tell I'm afraid she'll die before I do and it would absolutely kill me to lose her – so we'd better break up now. Do you think she'd buy that?

Anyway, she came for a ride on my car today. She didn't seem right from the moment she climbed on board. She kept jingling her bracelets – she has too many of them, if you ask me. She sat up in front near me and was jabbering on over her shoulder. It was something like: "The editing is malevolent. Trini keeps her hamster in a jar!"

I had no idea what she was talking about. "Are you okay?" I kept asking. She just ignored me and jabbered on, her eyes half wild, from what I could see "Darlene, are you having a stroke?" I asked her.

"No, are you?" she answered.

"You seem a little off," I said.

"But the little hamster!" Darlene said, getting quite perturbed.

"Who's Trini? He keeps his hamster in a jar?"

"No, no! You don't understand!" Darlene replied. "I am just so exhausted."

She did look exhausted, dark circles under her eyes. I wondered if she was even older than the 58 she admitted to. Not that I cared that much that she was an "older woman." "Do you want me to call somebody?" I asked.

"Who would you call?"

"An ambulance?"

She ignored me and just shook her bracelets some more. I kept expecting her to snap out of whatever it was she was in. But she didn't. "I'm going to call an ambulance," I threatened.

"I don't need an ambulance. Trini has margins out to here!" she went on.

"In his thesis?"

"I gobbled a liverwurst pretzel for lunch."

"Darlene, honey, I'm calling you an ambulance."

"I am not an ambulance!" she shouted. She shook her bracelets at me but wouldn't look at me.

I stood up and signaled to Gustavo, my conductor that day. "Could you call an ambulance? I think my girlfriend is having a stroke," I said.

He got out his cell phone and dialed. I think he has the number on speed dial, since we do need paramedics and such from time to time. Before you could say boo, an ambulance was roaring its way toward the cable car. I stopped not far from the Bohemian Club, and waved at the ambulance driver, a kid in his twenties wearing oversized sunglasses. Six different staff jumped out of the ambulance after it stopped next to us and clambered onboard.

"Hey, what's happening?" Darlene said as they began to surround her.

"What's your name?" a female paramedic asked her.

"What is this?!"

"Who called us?" one of them asked.

"I called for him," Gustavo answered, pointing at me.

"Who is she to you?" I was asked.

"She's my girlfriend," I said.

"What's her name?"

"Darlene."

The male doctor (or whatever he was) took over and grabbed Darlene by her shoulders. "What's your name, M'am?"

"I'm not telling you! Leave me alone!" Darlene said back.

Already the ambulance crew was readying a blue stretcher, while coming up behind Darlene, trying to catch her unawares.

"Is she violent?" one of them asked me. "Did she hit her head?"

"No, she just suddenly got sort of dingey," I replied.

"You'd better come with us, lady," another paramedic ordered.

"You leave me alone. This is absurd," Darlene countered. Her eyes met mine, and she seemed to be imploring me to not let them take her away.

"They just want to check you out, honey," I said.

"I'm not going. This is crazy," Darlene sort of mumbled as they fitted the blue stretcher around her and tilted her backward.

"You might be having a stroke, honey," I comforted her.

"Where are you, lady?" the male doctor (or whoever) inquired again. Darlene didn't reply this time, mostly out of stubbornness.

"She's non-responsive to my questioning," the doc decided.

They finished putting the blue stretcher around my Darlene and whisked her off the cable car and into the back of the ambulance. The passengers, about fifteen of them, rushed over to one side to watch her disappear into the vehicle. They'd have a story to tell when they got back home!

"Does she have medical insurance?" somebody asked me.

"I believe so. I'm not sure."

They looked through Darlene's purse until they found her insurance card. "Okay, we can go now!" a voice called out.

At the end of my shift, a couple of hours later, I went to the hospital where they'd taken her, Ralph K. Davies on Divisadero, and found Darlene in a little side room near the Emergency Room. I tiptoed in.

"Fuck you," she said when she saw me.

(That's all the thanks I got for saving her life.)

CR ED

I suppose I ought to mention that I had a girlfriend before Darlene. "The term "girlfriend" is misleading, however. Yeah, we had a kid together, but I barely knew the woman. If that is hard to believe, just let me say that she was actually more of stalker than a girlfriend. She was this big American Indian gal about thirty who wore her black hair parted in the middle and was fond of flowers next to the part, usually white magnolias. Her teeth were very good, but she was blind. I think she had been blind from birth. She had not let her blindness stop from pursuing her dream – even stalking her dream! Apparently something in my voice attracted her interest the first time she rode my cable car. Whatever the reason, she started riding almost every day, sitting right behind me in the first seat. I learned somewhere along the way that I was not the first cable car operator who had won her heart. She had had a kid with him too, and given it away.

I don't really mean to make fun of the poor woman. After all, she was blind, and I imagine her opportunities for meeting a mate were limited. I'm sure my voice is as sexy as hell, but she probably was just trying to know where the man she was interested in would be every workday. She could wait at the stop, ask who the driver was, and then hop on or off as she wished.

I said no at least six times when she asked me to "go out." I tried to be polite and sensitive to her feelings, but she kept asking. I was weak. I was young (sort of young: 42), and I was horny. Men do lots of things they shouldn't because they're horny.

She lived in a squalid little studio on Jones Street. She had made attempts to pretty it up, with fake flowers in some vases, an Oriental rug on the floor. But the place also smelled of old pet food. She apologized and said that her cat, Taffy Luv, had died recently and she hadn't really cleaned up yet. Yes, she was heart-breaking in almost every way. Except that she was always very chipper and always great sex. We did it thirteen times. I counted. I knew it couldn't last.

Out of the blue, one day she told me not to come back anymore. She did not tell me that she was pregnant. Sure, sure, I should have used a rubber. I did sometimes. But they make it hard to come, at least for me. I also very clearly asked her if she objected to me not using a rubber. She did not. Maybe she wanted a baby? It is surprising that more people don't seem to realize that babies come when a man and a woman fuck like rabbits. All those crappy movies where the man is so Surprised at the News!

Even I was surprised at the news. Only I didn't learn it until about a year after she told me not to come back anymore. She happened to get on my cable car, this time carrying a small boy. Another woman was with them, probably from Child Services, or whatever it is called. I suspected that the boy was mine. But she did not speak to me. And I did not speak to her.

I never saw her again.

Maybe the little ghost boy I thought was from 1909 was actually my son with the blind woman? . . . What bullshit. People love bullshit.

؃ ؄

Believe it or not, there was an occasional white guy on my cable car. One in particular I remember was this one who said he was from Rhode Island. Only he didn't have a New England accent. Maybe all of them don't? Maybe I've seen too many Pepperidge Farms commercials?

Whatever! He said he was forty-eight, and he may have been. Yet he was a roly-poly butterball who looked about ten years old. He was always hyper-agitated. Maybe he was on speed. Maybe he was just naturally jittery. Maybe it was a combination of the two. He tended to wear short pants and a baseball cap and constantly fed his face. He was the type that seems to enjoy making lots of noise opening his bags of corn nuts or trail mix. He also carried a half gallon liquid container and swigged after every other bite. He said it was spring water from a mysterious well high in the Himalayas. Maybe it was gin? He was always offering me a bite or a swig, but I politely declined.

I don't think this guy worked. He probably was on SSI. He liked to sit right next to me and chat away, turning around a lot, even when I was trying to concentrate on the tracks ahead. He usually asked me and the conductors not to examine his Fast Pass. He used an old one, months out of date.

He said he'd had a book published when he was nineteen and that it had sold 100,000 copies. It was about going to his high school prom with his teddy bear as his date. I couldn't tell if he was bullshitting me or not.

He was sort of fun, all things considered, always jumping up and running around on the cable car, talking to the other passengers, waving giddily at people on the sidewalk. He was just short of crazy. "Look at that goofy person!" he would often say, pointing at somebody else that we were passing. Believe me, he was right. There were plenty of 'borderlines' out there. He just didn't seem to see himself in the same light.

He said he was signing up to go make visits to middle school classes in San Francisco public schools. "To show them how to empathize with people like me," he explained. He also complained about having to take an eight-hour tutorial on how to "reach marginal, underserved students." "They want us to describe ourselves for two minutes. Two minutes are not enough! They also said there may be no questions from the students and we should be prepared for that. "Do you want to go with me?"

I didn't.

"Don't you want students to be more sympathetic to the marginal?" he asked in an accusatory way.

I bit my tongue and didn't say, "Don't be surprised if they beat the shit out you."

"Are you judgmental" he asked me one day.

"Never," I lied.

"I can tell you think I'm weird," he said. He was throwing corn nuts into air and trying to catch them with his open mouth – missing every bite.

"I am less judgmental than the Almighty," I said cryptically.

He grinned. "God speaks to me sometimes."

"Does He? . . . What does He say?"

"She said that I should get very fat. This was about six years ago."

"So you're just following God's will?" I said.

"I used to weigh one hundred pounds." He ran his hands up and down his rotundity. He was clearly in the two-fifty range now.

"We all weigh one hundred pounds at some time or other," I countered.

"Are you angry with me because I have grown fat?"

"No. Though I doubt that God told you to become that way."

"She did! She appeared to me in a bakery on Polk Street and said, "Arthur, partake of my many cakes and brownies. Have an apple fritter a day."

"No shit?"

"So I try to shoplift something from a bakery every day."

"And you don't get caught?"

"Oh, sure, I get caught all the time. I'm 5150!"

"Maybe you'd better stop, or at least try some new bakeries."

"I've run out of bakeries, I'm afraid."

"I think some bakeries throw out stuff, if you wait, and if you don't mind eating day old."

"I tried that, and it worked. Then I got the runs. Terrible pains in my tum tum."

"Your tum tum?"

He pointed to his stomach. "My teddy bear got sick too last year and died."

This went on for several years, and then Arthur didn't show up much on my cable cars. I learned eventually that he had hanged himself, or it may have been an accident. The clothes hook on his vest's collar got snagged on the edge of a metal dumpster as he was trying to find food, and he choked to death before he could get free. Perhaps God was calling Arthur to Him, in Her mysterious way.

CG 8O

I gave them names because I didn't know their real ones. The tall man I called Stanislaw, not to his face, of course. He must have been six-six with a hangman's droopy, mean face and meat-hook hands. His mother was bent over with osteo-something or other and crept along like a sick snail. She always had on a babushka with a cigarette dangling out of her mouth as she watched herself walking carefully so that she wouldn't slip and fall. I called her Madame Smokeyourassoff. No matter how many times I told her there was no smoking on the cable car, she ignored me and swore something at me in Russian (I think). It could have been Polish.

I wondered, vaguely, about their sex life. Did they still Do It? How long had they been married? They still talked to each other; that was something. How many couples had I seen that hadn't a syllable left to share?! The man was particularly attentive, fussing and fetching on the wife's behalf, offering her his sunglasses, even a flask that he kept in a back pocket. I think it probably was vodka. He seemed pretty bombed all the time. She muttered under her breath at him and took cash out of her wallet every so often and counted it out, very slowly. Then she would hand some money to her husband and he would put it in his cap. I guess he figured he was too tall for anybody to jump up and steal that cap with the money inside.

They both seemed to carry black clouds over their heads all the time. Sorry, but I've seen it a lot in people from that part of the world, who are dark, depressed and depressing, with a world view that couldn't be less like most Americans'. Americans are like puppy

dogs: "Oh, isn't that great! Look, isn't that going to be delicious! I wuv you so very much! Pet me! Pet me! "
The Russians are like this: "Life is deeply miserable. I hate being alive, and I vill kill you with this knife I carry in the back of my throat if you look at me again!"

God knows what horrors they had been through before coming to San Francisco. I think I heard the husband say one time that he'd had to go on a rickety old bus for four hours each way to get two pounds of meat. And half of that was rotten!

I suppose it should have made me sympathetic, but it didn't, not really. They were utterly without charm. You just knew they had an old, filthy bed with a big hole of an indentation in it, where they snored and slobbered on one another.

They didn't like me either. I'd see them "discussing" me from time to time, when they thought I wasn't watching. The old wife even mocked the way I pulled on the track brake, as if I were jacking off. I sort of hoped a passenger would steal her money when she counted out her bills to her old man. Or maybe the little ghost boy from 1909 would knock her off the car! (That's my boy!)

No, it wasn't pretty. They brought out the worst in me. You see all kinds on the cable cars, but these two didn't have a glint of anything warm or kind or out-going about them; maybe they had been in a "gulag." Or something. They seem more interesting now that I have written about them than any time I actually saw them in person. Funny about that.

The only "story" I have about the two, I guess, is when I saw the husband without the wife two times in a row. More to be mean than anything else, I asked, "How's your lovely wife doing?"

He looked at me with an even more desolate look than normal and said. "She died in our bed. And she was my Momma, not my wife!"

Oops. Eww!

CB BO

I saw my first Naked Guy on a cable car the other day. He may have been a refugee from the Castro Area, where certain members of the Outraged had come together to ban the presence of such unseemly flesh. Frankly, I don't especially want to see naked guys, in particular this one on my cable car: boney, saggy, and flabby. (Or were those three of the original Ten Dwarves but left out by Disney?!) He also had loose tits and a big, ugly nose. His feet weren't great either. Maybe he was proud of his Miraculous

Member? It was okay, but nothing to jump up and down about. He even put a newspaper under his butt, either to protect himself from public germs or to spare us his skid marks on the seat. (It gave a whole new meaning to the term Skid Row.)

He didn't say anything to me, and I didn't say anything to him. Some of the folks on the cable car seemed upset that he was there, sitting facing out toward the sidewalk. But they seemed more giggly embarrassed than deeply upset. He had brought a thermos full of coffee, it seemed. He kept taking swigs. I hope his bladder was in good shape. I wasn't optimistic about his insides, to judge from his exterior.

Everybody rode along, with the usual gettings-on and gettings-off. Some people were still covering their mouths and giggling, especially the Asians. At least two jumped up and took photographs of Mr. Naked. Then they all looked at the images on somebody's smart phone and giggled some more. I was surprised they didn't sit on his lap and pose for more pictures.

I thought it would blow over, and the Naked Guy would hop off and be on his way. But a young mother with a boy child who was just learning to walk got on, and a lot of the passengers suddenly took great umbrage. "Protect that baby!" a male voice cried out. "Cover his eyes!"

"Cover his eyes!" another voice shouted.

"Cover your private parts, Mister!" a grouchy old lady demanded. Five of them got up and surrounded the Naked Guy, as if to shield the poor baby from the sight of a penis.

All in all, there was a great to-do, and eventually the Naked Guy did something horrible.

Let me see if I can remember what it was.

He grabbed that baby and stuck his Miraculous Member in its ear!

No, that wasn't it.

He took the baby from the mother's begging arms and tossed it from the cable car, where it perished under ten imported automobiles on the streets of San Francisco.

No, that wasn't it, either.

Oh, now I remember. The little baby boy actually saw the naked penis when the nudist got up and pushed his way out through all the way to the back before he got off. I believe it even swung back and forth several times – the penis, not the baby. And he "got off" the cable car, not any other meaning of "got off." Maybe he "got off" on spooking the clothed?

Whatever. For the rest of its life that baby never recovered and was never the same, for he grew up believing that human beings actually had GENITALS underneath their clothes!

What a thing for people to get so worked up over!

CB 80

Don't blame me for this next story. I'm just the messenger.

Her name was Josie. His name was "Rosie." That wasn't his real name, just a family nickname. The real name, I heard, was Francis Xavier Hurley. These two were brother and sister, two years apart. They had grown up in the Mission District as good Roman Catholics. He was a scrappy tough kid with not an ounce of fat on his short, wiry Irish body. Always in fights and scrapes and pranks. His idea of a prank was to set fire to Father Hobart's vestments – not when he was actually wearing them, but when he had laid them out for Mass the night before. So "Rosie" the boy was quite a handful. He just seldom got caught. His sister Josie was a plainer version of the same genes, pale skin, too many freckles, wide mouth, a lurker –

always seeming to be hanging around, yet shy, watching everybody.

They were in their early thirties when they rode on my cable cars. "Rosie" worked in an automobile repair shop in North Beach. Josie often went up to meet him for dinner and a movie. They didn't seem to have any other friends. (I can relate.)

Then one night, the way people do, "Rosie" up and murdered some woman he had picked up in a bar in North Beach. They found her body off a pier along the Embarcadero. It was pretty bad, with forty-five slashes and stab wounds to the poor woman's face, neck, and body. She was a waitress who worked at "Beach Blanket Babylon" at Club Fugazi. Apparently she was just out for a good time after her dog had died, and she happened to run into "Rosie," and that was the end of her.

He had been seen with the victim by several other women witnesses, evidently women he had tried to pick up at the same bar but without success. They considered themselves very lucky and described "Rosie" to a T. He was arrested, never got out on bail, went to trial, and was given the death penalty. Swift Justice, it seemed.

But his sister did not believe a word of it. She just "knew" that her beloved brother could not be guilty of such a heinous crime. She therefore decided to get him out of prison before he was actually 'lethally injected,' as they say. The trouble was the sister had no legal training whatsoever. She had not even finished her B.A. degree. So she had to go to City College and finish her undergraduate requirements, transfer to SF State, and then get into law school.

That's when I saw the most of her, as she was riding my cable car to Hastings, working on her law degree. She always had big, heavy books with her, and she would pore over them, taking lots of notes, eventually needing glasses, getting mousier and mousier the closer to forty she got. But, boy, you had to give her credit. She was not going to let her brother's life be snuffed out. She showed me pictures of the two of them at various ages, at nine, then twelve, then in their mid-teens, on and on. She had given up everything else in her life, clearly, just so she could get her brother out of San Quentin. The funny thing was that she could see Alcatraz from some places on the cable car. "I'm getting Rosie out of that awful place!" she told me, pointing at Alcatraz as if it were San Quentin. A symbol is a symbol, I suppose. "Once I become a lawyer, I will have more access to everything," she said.

"Well, good luck to you," I told her. (I thought she had about as much chance as a snowball in Haiti.)

Life went on, as it often does, with nary a sign of dear, devoted, plain Josie, and, to tell the truth, I forgot about her. Then one day there was a news report about her and her brother. It seems that she had indeed gotten her law degree, became her brother's keeper (or at least his attorney), and was able to access forensic evidence that the police had mislabeled and misplaced at the Hall of Justice. She had to petition the courts and the attorney general of California and God knows who else to get a new trial. Former witnesses recanted some of their incriminating testimony about "Rosie," and even his DNA was shown not be match to what was on the dead woman's body. The murder weapon, a knife presumably, had never been recovered, and most likely was at the bottom of the Bay.

The brother wasn't exactly helpful, rumor had it, refusing to submit to a DNA test for half a year, causing dustups with some of the guards at San Quentin, finding himself in solitary confinement, and even attempting to hang himself with a bed sheet. But somehow he managed to get through it all.

His sister turned out to be a very good lawyer and was tenacious in pursuing justice for "Rosie." After years and years of trying, she finally got him out of San Quentin after his second trial, where he had been found Not Guilty by reason of insufficient evidence. The judge let him go immediately.

That should have been the end of the story: The brother released, finding a loving wife, raising two beautiful red-headed kids, getting a big financial settlement from the state for false imprisonment; the sister going on to a fabulous career with the Innocence Project, marrying Barry Schecht, freeing the guiltless, and also being rich enough to have lots of plastic surgery on her face.

Alas, none of that was to happen.

Nine months to the day after "Rosie" got out of prison, he stabbed and slashed his own sister to death in their apartment on Lombard Street – yes, that part they call the Crookedest Street in the World. It seems "Rosie" had a terrible, terrible temper. The newspaper reports were graphic, as was "Rosie's" last trial. It came out that Josie had been murdered in what was termed a "lovers' quarrel." So much for gratitude. (Is it not the smallest organ in the human brain?)

I've pretty much seen it all, but this one got to me. Yikes. The Triumph of the Human Spirit and all that. (And I thought my life was bad!)

 C3 80

Mr. Lo rode my cable cars every Thursday at eight A.M. for years. It began after his wife of many years died. "She was from the lower classes," he always reminded me. I didn't know whether to congratulate Mr. Lo or to commiserate. He himself spoke rather good English and may even have been a barrister in Shanghai back in the day. He was ninety-two now, with bad knees, a bad back, two canes, a bald head, false teeth, and a big smile. Unfortunately, he also always had a long nose hair sticking out of his left nostril, and it wasn't a dry hair either. He was quite chatty, and sat sideways, and I chatted away with him, but to be honest I couldn't look at his face most of the time, because of that slimy nose hair. I realize that is very superficial of me. But, really, who wants to look at a nose hair?!

Mr. Lo was very nosy and judgmental, always commenting under his breath about the "lower classes" who rode on public transportation in San Francisco. "I have found them to be of criminal intent," he said on many occasions. "Because they are threatening, I will not ride on your public transportation, except this cable car, where I can get off in a hurry," he told me. Sometimes he stomped his two canes on the floor to emphasize his point. I could only agree with him. "In Shanghai the lower classes do not misbehave!" he said proudly. (Maybe so, but

I'm still not moving there. I think they actually forbid immigrants, as a matter of fact.) I knew he was talking about blacks. It was pretty evident to me that the Chinese felt no White Guilt whatsoever and would have gladly sent all criminals to Re-education Camp.

Mr. Lo got more and more bent over as the years passed. "I look like I have worked in the rice fields!" he lamented. Indeed he did. "I think I do not have much longer on this earth," he told me one day.

"Of course you do!" I lied, giving him two phony thumbs up. Yeah, on some days I realize that I don't have to say everything I think, just play the part of the smiling cable car flunky.

"My daughter says that I will outlive her!" he cackled. "Believe me, I am trying!"

"Do you live with your daughter?" I asked him.

"Oh, Lord, no!" he said. "She orders me around as if she were Chairman Mao."

"But she does look in on your from time to time, yes?" I wondered.

"She used to, but I told her not to come anymore."

"No!"

"But yes!" he said. "I do much better without the stress of her."

I wanted to ask if he didn't get lonely, with both his wife and daughter gone from his life.

"I am not lonely," he answered my unasked question. "Better to be alone than to be unhappy with your family!"

"Is that Confucius?" I asked.

"No, it's me! If you ask me, Confucius is often wrong." He did not laugh.

"There are senior services that look in on people," I said. "I can get you some phone numbers if you like."

"Thank you. I would appreciate that."

But you know how things get. I was too busy with my own problems and my job, and I did not get those numbers for Mr. Lo. I gradually saw less and less of him.

It was only by happenstance that I learned that the man had died. There was a small obituary of him in a Chinese newspaper that somebody had left on my cable car. I recognized Mr. Lo's face and name. He had been rather prominent back in his homeland, it seemed. He was scheduled to be laid out for a public viewing a few days hence.

When I got to the Xiang Peace Parlor, I was the only one there, except for the female funeral director and Mr. Lo, of course. He was lying in a nice walnut casket with plenty of purple padding, dressed in a good brown suit and drab necktie. I don't know if it was an oversight or deliberate, but the nose hair was still there. Maybe nose hairs don't bother other people as much as they bother me. At least it was dry now.

I knelt next to his body. "I'm sorry you died alone," I whispered to him. "I hope it doesn't happen to me."

And then, yes, I clipped that nose hair and threw it away at Ocean Beach and sent Mr. Lo on to meet the upper classes in the Next Whatever.

og &o

The Giants have won several World Series. And I have been a big fan, or at least a fair-weather fan. When they lose, I run the other way. My girlfriend, Darlene, says I am disloyal to my team. I think she really means to her. She has confused our relationship with my interest in the Giants. As I said, she may not even be my girlfriend anymore. I haven't heard from her since I had her carted off by the paramedics and she told me to fuck off.

I'm not calling her! Say la vie? Is that how you spell it? Why do I always have to be the one to make up? It's long past her turn.

Anyhow, it was great that the Giants were the world champs, although the team was made up of people from anywhere but San Francisco and they all are probably off to other teams by the time I write this! You take what you can get, I suppose, by way of celebrations.

We had a lot of "celebrating" fans on the cable cars, both the night of the clincher and even the next day a little bit. What assholes! Where did they get the idea that setting a cable car on fire with old rags and sticks was good for anybody or anything? I personally had to put out two fires myself. And the assholes threatened me for doing so! They were drunk, and I'm not supposed to have noticed. When I started this journal, I told myself that I wanted to write "uplifting" tales of the cable cars, but the fact of the matter is a lot of what happens there is not uplifting. In fact, it's a downer.

"Man, you tryin' to keep us from havin' a good time?" one of the assholes yelled at me. He was in "uniform" – black and orange jacket, black and orange baseball cap, sideways, of course. Big and Fat and no doubt from The Mission. He would have looked like a jerk, if he wasn't so threatening.

"Yeah, that's exactly what I'm trying to do!" I yelled back.

"Who 'pointed you God?"

"God did! Fuck you." He had a heavy accent, but I wasn't supposed to notice that either. "Go back where you came from!" I said.

"I'm gonna report you, man, to the authorities!"

"Yeah, well, show 'em your green card at the same time, gringo!" Hell, I was in deep already, so what the fuck! "You think you're improving the area with your goddamned 'diversity,'" I went on. It galls the hell out of me that I have to kiss assholes' asses!

"I have a right to be here! What's your name, dude?"

"Benjamin Franklin."

"Well, Benjamin, let's see if you have your job after I get through to your boss."

"Yeah, well, we have free speech here in America!" (Why did I say that? Of course we don't have free speech here if it's about "ethnicity." Unless you are trashing whites.)

"It's just a little fire, man. Get over it."

"It's not just the fire. It's your fucking numbers, you selfish, overpopulating fucking Catholics with your endless kids, who do badly in school! Fuck you! Fuck you! You bring nothing to this country but trouble!"

"We're gonna bury you!" I was informed.

"Oh, go shoot somebody because he's wearing red instead of blue." I waved my free hand at him. "Beat up a gay!"

"Man, you *are* angry!" He seemed genuinely surprised.

"Because I see fuckheads like you destroying my world, and we were all too pussy to say anything or do anything about it. Well, not this time, not this time! Not all immigrants are good! Not by a long shot!"

He came closer to me, with a lighted stick in his hand. "Yeah? What are you going to do about it here?" He spat on the floor of the cable car.

"I'm going to summon the little boy from 1909 and have him push you off the cable car?"

"What?!"

"Failing that, I am going to see that you all self-deport yourselves by next year."

"Huh?"

"Oh, another low-information voter!" I screamed.

"You'd better simmer down, dude, and drive this cable car right. I paid my fare."

"No, you didn't! You jumped on, did not pay, and then started a fire. Why am I not overjoyed to have you aboard?!"

"I'm gonna poke your eyes out with this stick."

"Where did you learn how to do that, in Citizenship Class?"

"I'm already a fucking citizen, asshole!"

"Then you shouldn't be. You are making San Francisco a fucking Third World country just like where you came from with your every breath. And your goddamned father thought he was so macho because he has ten or twelve kids, kids he can't even take care of!"

"I love America!"

"You do not love America!"

"I do too!"

"If you love America, you wouldn't set fires on the cable car!"

"It's one time, one time only! "Cause the Giants is the champs!"

"That's just an excuse! You can't even make the subject agree with the verb!"

We went on like that for a while. Then I strangled him with a Giants championship flag until his eyes bulged out and he died a horrible, horrible death and went to Hell.

Naw, I didn't.

I hadn't realized until that moment how much anger I had been keeping in. Road rage lives on the cable cars!

And, no, they didn't fire me because they couldn't trace any "Benjamin Franklin" in the cable car personnel. Ha! Fuck him. He didn't even know who Benjamin Franklin is!

ᗰ ᗷ

Yeah, I thought when I started this memoir about the cable cars, the stories would be a lot cheerier, you know, peppy and optimistic, like America. (Sort of stupid, actually.)

I just can't do it. Okay, let me try. Did you hear about the little crippled girl on the cable car who shared her Krispy Kreme raspberry donut on Christmas Eve with the homeless man that she thought was a too-skinny Santa Claus and saved his life? ... Gag. I used to tell this story to Darlene every year in the Holiday Season, and she loved it. Then one year I made the mistake of telling her that I had made it up, that not a word of it was true. Darlene didn't talk to me for two weeks and said that I had "ruined"

Christmas for her "forever." Christ! People love crap. I don't get it. Oh, I get it. I just don't want it.

Let's see if I can think of a Positive Story.

Okay, there was this guy named Horatio who used to ride the cable car a few years ago. I think he was an ESL teacher, a smart guy. About thirty-five then, black curls all over his head, a "noble" nose like a Roman emperor, worked out a little too much, to the point where he looked disproportionate in his upper body. I'm pretty sure he was gay. He told me a scary story about taking some guy home and waking up having been drugged and robbed. I don't know if that was the catalyst that sent him in a new direction or not. I don't mean straight. I mean that he became a priest. That's right, he became a Catholic priest. I saw him in his vestments conducting a wedding Mass for a couple I knew who got married in Bernal Heights. What was this Horatio doing up there on the altar, "officiating" and guiding his "flock"?! Did he really agree to be celibate so that he could guide a flock? That means no sex, right? And he was gay??? It means not even "pleasuring yourself," if I have my doctrines correct. Why would he want to become a Catholic priest, for God's sake? How could he live without sex? I get little enough from Darlene as it is. Who'd voluntarily give it up for some "flock" of sheep? Maybe I should become a priest!

I saw Horatio one day in his priestly garb, the white collar, the black suit. He was wearing schoolmarm eyeglasses as well, had become a bit chunkier all over. "Father Horatio?" I said.

"Father Guinino," he replied.

"How did this happen?"

"God summoned me."

"Really? Did he send a text?"

He laughed. "No, I saw it written in the sky."

He was joking, showing, I guess, that he didn't take himself too seriously.

"How's that celibacy workin' for you?" I asked.

"That's between my God and myself."

"Remarkable. You are the last guy I thought would go priest on me."

"I enjoy helping people with their spiritual needs."

"Yeah, so do I. But I ain't givin' up my orgasms! They are few and far between as it is!"

"People have different needs at different times in their lives."

"I guess. It seemed to happen rather fast, didn't it?"

"I had been mulling it over for some time. I already had a Master's degree and a Catholic upbringing, so getting the ordination wasn't that difficult."

"Do you really believe all that crap, Virgin Birth and Immaculate Conception and so on?"

"All jobs you may want have parts that you are not especially fond of. I find that not too many of my parishioners come to me with questions about the Immaculate Conception. They are more personal. They usually need someone to confide in."

"People try to confide in me sometimes here on the cable car, but I make them get off at the next stop." I laughed.

"Different strokes for different folks," he said.

"Don't they know you're gay? You are gay, right?"

"I was gay. I thought it over and agreed to put sex out of my life. I took a vow."

"I would never take a vow with some company that made me give up sex, not even MUNI and its cable cars!"

"Well, people are not all the same."

I knew I was pushing it. It was, after all, his business, not mine. I was just so dumb-founded by his decision, that's all. "What if you are tempted by sin?"

"I have my breviary. That keeps me busy. If fluid builds up, it comes out while I sleep."

"What fun is that?!" I argued.

"You're looking at me as if I'm crazy. Let me just say this. I used to worry about my looks all the time, about going to the gym, looking for handsome tricks. I had plenty, by the way. Then one day I realized that I had had my share of such things. It was now time to worry about other people. And that's what I do these days. I never have a depressing day, even when I have people with depressing problems. I don't solve everything, not by a long shot, but I do manage to make people feel better, to offer comfort. It is amazing just how many people merely need a little comfort in their lives in order to go on."

We were coming to the turnaround at Powell and Market, so I had to stop the conversation. I nodded at Father Ex-Gay and smiled him on his way. I am sure that he was a wonderful help to people in his new role. God bless him.

Now as for the next part of this story. I don't know if it undermines the whole story or makes it a positive one: about a month after I saw him on my cable car he got run over by a big SUV on Leavenworth Street and died at the scene. He had been comforting a wino lying in his own vomit and jay walked against a red light trying to hail a passing cop car. I'm sure Father Guinino is in Heaven.

(I just don't think there's a Heaven.)

附 ⁊

An old flame of mine from years ago, Ramona Gershewitz, was riding on my cable car today. We were an item some twenty years ago, when I was about thirty and she was fifty. Yeah, I like older women. You got a problem with that? Unfortunately, Ramona didn't recognize me. She has gone a little ga-ga. More than a little, actually.

I turned around and there she was in the compartment behind me: her dyed red hair looking a little sparse in the front, her face-lift a bit past its prime, shall we say. Too much make-up. For God's sake, lady! She had bulked up as well, and I think her knees were bothering her. She kept stroking them. I tried to make eye contact, but she was not cooperating. Maybe she was still mad at me, from when we broke up. Ramona could hold grudges, big time. She didn't speak to either of her sons for years when they tried to get her to sign some property over to them to manage, because she herself was managing it badly. She seemed to think her boys were trying to take advantage of her. They weren't, I'm pretty sure. One of them had even called me after Ramona and I broke up to try to get me to get her to sign a Power of Attorney. I sent her a letter asking about it but never heard back. Maybe she had moved.

I would hear things about Ramona over the years: she was on a safari in Tanzania with a group of Episcopalian lady missionaries – or she would have been if she had managed to get her passport renewed in time. She had waited until the day before they were to leave to renew the passport. Of course by then it was too late. She had also asked some Swedish man to marry her after she met him in a jazz club in North Beach and pestered him with her "Hello, Gorgeous: Love Poems from Sven" (These were poems she wrote to *herself* as though they were from Sven) He left the country.

Ramona had indeed been gorgeous in her heyday. Now she looked . . . how shall I put it? Not gorgeous. It wasn't her fault unless refusing to walk anywhere and eating every chocolate truffle in sight for seventy years was somebody else's fault! Naturally, she dieted just as often. Up and down she went: the Adkins diet, the Jenny Craig, the Weight Watchers, the all-raspberry diet, the oyster crackers and split pea soup diet, the Dachau diet. (Okay, I made up some of these!) The point is she had no common sense. She did have a Ph.D., a fact she never failed to remind me of. "You need to go back to school," she'd lecture me. "You're not going to be able to steer those cable cars forever, you know." She wasn't exactly raking in the dough with her Ph.D. She was an adjunct at San Francisco State in the ESL Department, just barely getting by. "We'll see who outlasts who," I used to tell her, pissing her off no end.

"More education would improve your conversation," she'd tell me.

"My conversation's just peachy as it is!" I'd say back.

"Don't you want to expand your mind to the universe?"

Oh, for Christ's sake, her Ph.D. was in education! She wrote her "dissertation" on how gypsy argot was a legitimate branch of English and should be taught in American schools, or some such crap. And she's telling me to get more "education"?! At least I got my high school diploma when it actually meant something!

I hesitated about whether to speak to her on the cable car this time. Finally, when we stopped for a line of cars in front of us, some fender-bender, I went back and stood next to Ramona. "You remember me?" I said.

Her eyes, semi-closed and dozing, opened, and she turned her head toward me. "Ed?" she asked.

"No, not Ed," I replied.

"Rufus?"

"No, not Rufus."

"Were you a student of mine?"

God, she really didn't remember me! She was that far gone into senility. "We used to be friends," I said.

"Oh, I don't think so, Mister."

Was this going to happen to me? Not being able to remember somebody you'd had sex with, had shared bodily fluids with?! "So how are you, Ramona?" I managed.

"You know my name?"

"It was a long time ago. It's not important. How are you doing these days?" I knew I'd have to get back to my station at the front pretty soon.

"Oh, I am doing splendidly!" She positively perked up, eyes all a-buzz. "I just had some very good news." She held up a large envelope.

She looked like she could use some good news. "That's great!" I said. "Do you mind sharing it with me?"

"Oh, I can't share with money with you!" she explained. "It's my money and I don't know you." She put the envelope into her purse.

I almost patted her hand, the way I had in the past when she said silly things. "I don't expect you to give me money, Ramona. I'm doing fine financially."

She checked me out to see if I was telling the truth, still not recognizing me. Then suddenly she did seem to remember. "Oh, you're what's his name!" she said. "You went on the Pritikin diet with me, didn't you?"

I admitted that I had.

"That was a very good diet," she said.

"I guess it was."

"I lost thirty-seven pounds on that. And I kept it off for eighteen months." She nodded, mostly to herself, sagaciously. "I should try that again."

"Well, it was nice seeing you, Ramona," I said, starting to leave.

She tugged at my shirt sleeve a little. "I just have to tell somebody about my good luck." She smiled. I could see some of the old (or young) Ramona in that smile when she did. She had always been kind-hearted, and even when we argued she didn't get nasty, the way I or Darlene could.

"And what is that?" I encouraged her.

"I am in the final stages of my negotiations with my benefactors."

"Oh?"

"They are sending me the third set of contracts to sign."

"Contracts?"

"It's a huge amount of money that they will be sending me, so everything has to be just so."

"Ramona, you didn't . . . you haven't . . . ?"

"Now don't be like my sons. All they do is scream at me. But they're just jealous. They can't stand the fact that I know how to make as much as they do. My son's a dentist, did you know? The other one makes porn videos. He doesn't think I know that, but I do. He is the producer, not the actor."

"Ramona, who are these people you are going to give your money to?"

"It's this financial group in Jamaica called Help Boomers Bloom. They discovered that I have inherited ten and half million U.S. dollars, and they are clearing the way to send it to me by next month."

I'm afraid my jaw dropped, literally.

"Isn't that wonderful?" she went on. "As a bonus, I also get twenty-seven roundtrip airline tickets to anywhere in the world. But I can barely use so many. Would you like one? I could bring it to you when I get mine."

"Oh, no," I said.

"You aren't going to scream at me too?" Ramona said, looking as if I might hit her.

My heart went out to her. "Of course not. But I don't think any Jamaicans are going to send you twenty-seven airline tickets."

"Oh, but they are! And roundtrips one at that!" She rocked back and forth on the cable car seat in anticipation.

"Ramona!" I said with some anguish in my voice.

"Don't you dare try to stop me! I am only seventy-one and I still want to fly around the world. I have not even been to Turkey yet!"

"Ramona . . ." I was at a loss for words.

"It's not a scam. Those Jamaicans are my friends. When I taught, I was especially fond of my Jamaican students. It is not a scam!"

"How much money have you sent them?" I asked.

"None of your business."

"How much?"

"A little."

"Where are you getting the money from if you are retired?"

She shook her head, but then answered immediately, as if bragging. "I took some from my pension."

"Not from the principal?"

"You've got to trust people. I will get the money back, many times over."

"Ramona, it may not be my business, but we were . . . friends once upon a time. You can't send your money to crooks in Jamaica or anywhere else." I really needed to get back to driving the cable car.

"It's my money – despite what my sons seem to think. I got the Power of Attorney revoked, and they are never getting me to sign another one as long as I live!" Her face went red with determination.

"Ramona, no one is going to send you ten and half million dollars. Why would they?"

"It's their legal obligation, they say. And they are also my friends now."

"No, they're not. They are robbing you blind!"

"Says you!"

"Believe me, they don't want to give you money. They want *your* money!"

"You sound just like my sons!"

"Your sons are right. Don't you dare send those thieves any more money."

"But I've told them I am a retiree on a very fixed income. So they wouldn't do anything to harm me."

"Yes, they would. People are ruthless."

"I don't think that's true."

"I deal with the public. It's true!"

"They've even invited me to this resort they own in Belize for a two-week stay with all expenses paid, once we settle the paperwork on my inheritance."

I shook my head. "This is sad."

"You're the one who's sad," Ramona said. "I don't know how you get by being so cynical all the time."

"I'm not cynical! I'm realistic."

"Well, we'll just see, won't we? When I fly over this cable car and wave down to you on my way to Istanbul!" With that, Ramona got up and signaled for a stop. "Off to the bank now to get my final security deposit!"

I felt like I should follow her and stop her from throwing her money away. But I was at work and she was an old flame, and I was not my old flame's keeper. Or whatever.

I went back to my post. She slowly got off the cable car and then waved her envelope at me triumphantly. "You sucker!" were her final words to me as she hobbled toward her bank.

ᴄ8 ᴃᴐ

There was this TV show back in the day I've heard about: "There are eight million stories in the Naked City," something like that. I sorta feel the same way about my cable car stories. There are 800,000 stories in the City by the Bay! Of course most of the people riding don't have any story at all! Or at least I don't know what it is. Most people's stories that I have heard are likewise pretty flat at the end: "And then I dropped my peanut butter sandwich on my Barbie!" "The escaped gorilla ran off and didn't eat my face off!"

So I don't know if this next tale counts.

There was this elderly man, black, I believe, though after a certain age, it's hard to tell. You know what I'm saying: they get all sort of bleached out and blubbery and run-together in the face, with age spots like little burnt pancakes on their temples. He must have been eighty-five if he was a day, or perhaps he'd had a really rough life up to forty! He had the ugliest shoes I've ever seen on a human being: faded tan, dilapidated, and full of holes. He tended to wear a heavy raincoat, even when it wasn't raining, and looked like he had gastric distress a lot. I heard him fart a few times, but I pretended not to notice. He would sit up near the front, where I was, and shoot the breeze over his shoulder. I don't recall a single thing he said to me, except the very last thing he said, the last time he got off the cable car. (I'll get to that.)

He rode with me about once every three weeks or so. He got on and off at the same place every time, so I suspected he lived in one of those tiny, crummy apartments in the Tenderloin. He didn't look hungry or drunk or on drugs. He didn't talk to the other passengers, so far as I could tell. I never had the feeling that he was actually going anywhere. He was just riding the cable cars.

That last day I ever saw him he came closer to me and offered his hand. I didn't take it, nodding at the brake stick, meaning I had to keep both hands free. "Oh, I understand," the old guy said.

"See you next time," I said, trying to sound friendly even though I hadn't shaken his hand.

"I somehow doubt that I'll be back," he said. There was no self-pity in his voice, just a matter-of-factness that was chilling.

"Where are you going?" I asked.

"To the Big Cable Car Ride in the sky," he answered. He smiled. I smiled. (Why were we smiling?)

"Aw, you'll be back here. You watch!" I blustered.

He shook his head. "No. They detected something."

"Oh."(How lame was that? "Oh" is all I could muster up?)

"I just wanted to thank you."

"No need to thank me. I'm just doing my job."

"I wanted to thank you for talking to me over these years."

"Has it been years?"

"I've never had a family. My friends died off one by one some time ago. Somehow I just never made any new ones. Then I retired, and I didn't seem to know anybody anymore. So I'd go for weeks and weeks not talking to anybody, except the TV!" He gave a little laugh. "I always win the argument with the TV."

I was growing more and more uncomfortable.

"So thank you for talking to me when you did, providing me with some human connection. Of course the Arab gentleman at the corner grocery will talk to me sometimes, when he isn't busy or at closing time. But you are the one who has kept me going. You have been my best friend, and I want you to know I appreciate it."

And then he left, and I hadn't even shaken his hand or be able to remember a syllable he had ever said or even his name. Oh, my God, how sad is that?! (I've got to call Darlene and make up. I don't want to die like that.)

ʊ ʊ

There was this other loner that rode my cable car a lot. I think he worked as a waiter at some restaurant on Nob Hill that specialized in crepes. He might have been a dish-washer. I wasn't sure. He was about forty, slender, with a thin face and thinner hair, not especially ugly or handsome. He didn't say ever much to me, but I think one time he told me his name was Ari. To be honest, I didn't care what his name was. For God's sake, I see hundreds of people a day. Most of them I never see again. Ari, for all I knew, was one of the masses. Sorry to be so "elitist," but bite some reality, okay?

I will say this Ari looked Jewish. Can you say that? Oh, for God's sake, but nowadays you can't say this and you can't say that, even when it's obvious! Fuck it! I didn't say it was BAD to look Jewish! People come in all sizes and shapes, and plenty of them are dopes and shits. It's one thing to be against people because they're Jewish. That doesn't mean you have to like them because they're Jewish! Yet if I hear another word about the "situation in the Middle East" I swear I am going to puke. What do I think about the Middle East? Keep it over there, away from me. That ass won't wipe!

I suspect that many people carry around a secret, something they don't want anybody else to know. Maybe they masturbate to religious icons or whatever. Maybe they killed their parakeet when they were six. Probably most of these "secrets" aren't worth keeping, especially now that everybody is appearing on TV shows and bragging about their sins: "I had my pastor's bastard baby!" "I am addicted to organic lettuce!"

This Ari guy somehow seemed to carry around a secret. I would overhear him say something to somebody occasionally. But I didn't try to eavesdrop very hard to see what was what. I never saw him with anybody else. But then again, I thought, maybe he had a warm and lovely family back home, and he just rode the cable car to his job by himself because that's the way some folks get to their job, right?

Eventually I learned what Ari's secret was. There was a picture of him, some ten years earlier, when he was around thirty, in the newspaper. I seldom buy a paper, but they get left on the seats, so I glance at them now and then.

Apparently he had poured boiling hot water on his son when the kid was a baby. He had scalded the baby's face and legs – on purpose. It had to do with his divorce from his wife and a custody fight over their kid. Because she was getting the kid, the father scalded the hell out of his own baby! And he'd only served six years for it. My God. There was a photo of the kid too, all scarred and disfigured and blind in one eye even though the article talked about what "progress" the kid was making. Jesus Christ. I wished to hell I didn't know the guy's goddamned secret! Why do they put that stuff in the paper?!" It was supposed to be "uplifting"!

And then this Ari comes over to me that same day and says, "May I have a transfer, please?"

"No, you may not, not on the cable cars!" I yelled at him.

"Oh, you saw it," he said, looking sheepish.

"I did!"

He paused. "Well, in my defense, just let me say I wasn't aiming for the baby. I was aiming for my wife."

"What?! Get off my cable car!" I growled. "And we don't give transfers to anybody! But especially to you!"

He did get off, looking back at me with a terrible guilt in his dark eyes.

I got down on my knees that night and thanked God that I wasn't that guy. And I vowed that if Darlene and I made up, I'd never pee in her coffee cup when I'm mad at her again, which was my dirty little secret.

ୟ ଃ

Did I tell you that I have a pet rat? Probably not. I'm not supposed to have it on the cable cars, but, hell, it keeps me warm on those cold, foggy days. I call him Bitty. He is a white rat, which an ex-friend of mine rescued from a lab. He is about eight inches long, not counting the tail, with one ear that's ripped a little on the edge. I love his pink eyes. (I hope it's not conjunctivitis!) Usually he stays inside my MUNI jacket (not my shorts!) and especially likes just under my left armpit, but I have to wear an undershirt on the days when I bring Bitty with me to work. Otherwise, I get scratches from his claws. I have shown my rat to only a few riders, 'cause I'm afraid they'll turn me in for violating the rules. I've never understood why some people get so freaked out by rats, shrieking and carrying on like lunatics. Rats are much cuter than cats, and nicer too. Rats don't kill birds! Cats are cold and aloof and cruel. They kill rats for no reason except that they're rats. You don't see rats killing cats!

Darlene says I'm crazy. She's one of those people with a blind hatred of rats. She won't even come over to my place unless I swear on a thousand Bibles that Bitty is inside his cage. What a nuisance it is always having to find Bitty and lock him up just so Her Majesty Darlene will deign to place herself in my bed for a few minutes every once in a while. What we do for sex!

I might add that Darlene likes cats. She keeps giving hers names like "Cutesy" and "Wootsey," when the plain fact of the matter is her cats are criminals! I've seen them with my own eyes ripping some poor little hummingbird to shreds in Darlene's apartment. (She lets them come and go as they please.) The goddamn cats even took turns batting the hummingbird back and forth to each other, when they thought there was an ounce of life left in its tiny body. Darlene thinks her cats will be by her side when the Big One hits San Francisco, and they will all die together in each other's arms comforting each other. I tell her that, no, those cats will survive and feed off her dead body until they are rescued by the SPCA. Oh, Darlene will scold her cats sometimes – say if they bring in a live sparrow or a polar bear cub or whatever. But then she forgets and starts baby talking to "Cutesy" and "Wootsey" as if they aren't little serial murderers. It's a good thing that Darlene and I never had kids. She would have made them into overly entitled vicious monsters as sure as I live and breathe!

Excuse the rant. I realize that other people's pets are as uninteresting as other people's children!

Actually, I only mentioned my rat because something happened today. It got loose when we had a sudden jolt at Bay Street. Bitty fell out of my jacket, or jumped. He was running around the seats, and naturally some passengers saw him and freaked out. "A rat! A rat!" several screamed. I thought they were going to leap into on-coming traffic they looked so frightened. "Oh, get over yourself," I muttered.

I couldn't catch Bitty, although I came close a couple of times. He jumped up on my shoulder once, and I thought I had him securely in my hands. But then he scampered down my body and literally turned around and around in place, not knowing where to go. "Come here, boy," I said, tapping on the floor. He saw me but seemed too traumatized to move. I reached down to swoop him up, but just then some crazed anti-rat white lady let out a loud whoop, and Bitty, startled again, flew through the air. This time he fell off the cable car.

I managed to make my way to the edge of the car and looked down at the street and the tracks. I couldn't see him. "Bitty!" I called. Then I yelled: "BITTY!" After a few seconds, he poked his head out from underneath the cable car. His nose was twitching and he was shaking. He may have injured himself on the metal of the tracks or the asphalt. I reached down my hand. But he was too far away. Nobody offered to help. My conductor that day, Ron (the Asshole) was fussing with some passengers in the rear. Bitty was too scared to climb into my hand. He just crouched there, halfway out and halfway under the cable car.

Ron the conductor was up in front near me now, pissed as hell. "What the fuck are you doing?" he cursed at me. "Why don't you move the car?" He didn't wait for my answer and just unlocked the wooden brake. Which is against the rules!

"Wait!" I screamed.

But the cable car didn't wait. It lurched forward a foot or two.

"Ron, wait!

I heard Bitty let out a tiny squeak, and I looked back. Sure enough the cable car had run over Bitty's body. He probably could have moved away, but I guess he was too terrified to. One of his front legs was lying separated from his body. The cut had just begun to bleed. I clambered off the cable car as fast as I could. "Oh, my God," I said, looking down at Bitty's severed leg. I didn't know what to do. I stood there helpless. Bitty hadn't gone into shock and just looked up at me as if to say, "What happened? Can't you help me? You always help me, Big Guy." I took out my handkerchief and tried to stop the bleeding. I picked up the leg and put it in my shirt pocket. They can sew it back on, I thought to myself. If they can do it for a person, then can do it for Bitty. But the handkerchief was not enough, even though I wrapped it around Bitty's body and kept gently patting it. "Please don't go to sleep!" I whispered to him. His eyes were beginning to close. Like a fool, I gave him mouth to mouth resuscitation.

Everything I had ever learned about saving another life froze uselessly in my head.

And then Bitty just sort of fell to one side, away from me. He closed his eyes and didn't open them anymore. I knelt there in the street with a little rat blood on my lips, weeping as I had never wept before, weeping for Bitty, and weeping for my and Darlene's dying relationship and for San Francisco, and weeping for myself because I realized that the only thing in the whole world that I really, really loved was this dead rat.

"Oh, for God's sake, leave it!" Asshole Ron said, disgusted with me.

ೞ ೲ

Smoking is not allowed on the cable cars, in case you're interested. It's part of my job to police the smokers. I don't like policing anybody. If I wanted to do that, I'd have become a cop! Nevertheless, I have to make the passengers obey the law. Sometimes they resist. Usually they accept my rulings. People have flicked I don't know how many cigarettes, cigars, and cigarillos from my cable cars into the streets of San Francisco. What power I have!

But there was one middle-aged Italian gentleman who not only smoked on my car but liked to wave his stogies all over the place, sending clouds of cigar smoke in all directions, and nothing I said would dissuade him. He also liked to sing arias from various Italian operas in the original language, often coughing and choking in between verses. He was in a wheelchair and didn't have any legs, not even one. So it was a bitch getting him on and off the cable car, even with that handicapped access shit. It was easier just to let him stay and sing away. His hair was greasy and stringy with a large bald spot at the top. His face had seen better days, or maybe it hadn't. Let's just say he wasn't being asked to pose for calendars. He also hit passengers up for money. "I sing-a for you Puccini!" he liked to say, gesticulating. (Sorry if I'm "stereotyping"! As far as I can tell, "stereotyping" just means pointing out what's true, although certain people don't want you to notice anymore.) "If you like-a, you give-a me a dollar." Sorry, that's what he sounded like! He had what some might call an "infectious" smile – probably from bird flu or cholera, it was hard to tell. He probably made pretty good money from his "act." "I'm-a the great-grandson of the great Caruso!" he would proclaim. When asked what happened to his legs, he said, "I was part of a magic act and my boss got carried away!" Then he laughed, so I guess it wasn't true. Probably more likely he lost them in some war or other. There's always a war to lose your legs in. (Yeah, yeah, I support the troops. Only they should maybe be just a teensy weensy bit smarter about which wars they fight in. Just sayin'. Not all the ex-soldiers I encounter are nice, either.)

This one day the Opera Star was even more obnoxious than usual. I think he had added some *vino* to his repertoire. Isn't there a Drinking Song in some opera? I am afraid I don't know nothin' about opera. Anyway, Caruso Reborn was belting out a tune, cigar smoke wafting everywhere. The passengers were either fascinated or annoyed, or both. Suddenly an ember from the man's cigar fell onto his pants, just above where his legs should have been. There must have been kerosene or cleaning fluid or something on his clothing because he went up in flames in a few seconds. Several people tried to extinguish the fire, but nothing could be done. The Opera Star burnt to a crisp, and soon there was almost nothing left on the wheelchair.

You're right. That never happened. Too bad!

What really happened is that he is singing on my cable cars to this day, every week or so. I can't get him to not smoke his cigars, to not panhandle, and to not sing his goddamned opera. I even offered to give him twenty dollars if he would just ride and not sing. But he won't hear of it. "They love-a my singing!" he keeps telling me. "They applaud for me. You are a bastard and I am a great artist!"

It's true that people applaud. But my Opera Star is an absolutely terrible singer. Surely he has never heard his own voice. But, Buddy, the real and *only* reason people applaud is because you have no legs. . . It's called Show Biz!

℃ ℗

The irony of the next tale is not lost on me. I had the pet rat that I had to keep hidden until it died. At the same time I had to tell this elderly black woman named Lakeesha that she couldn't bring her pet dog on the cable cars. She said, "But it's a Seeing Eye dog." It was a lala ipso, or whatever the hell they're called – one of those little, pushed-in-face kind with tufts of whitish hair.

"But you're not blind," I scolded Lakeesha.

So she started pretending to be blind, feeling around with her hand whenever she saw me looking back at her. I knew the dog was in her handbag. Its head would pop out every now and again. If passengers saw it, they thought it was cute. So did my conductors. Nobody thought my rat was cute!

I think Lakeesha was a cleaning lady, somewhere up on Nob Hill. She must have made decent money. Well, at least she wasn't in rags. And she did have that lala ipso. Aren't they expensive? She kept herself clean and together, although her coat might have been from 1955. She wore it all the time. She had one of those faces that could be forty or eighty with a little too many lines on it.

One day, for the umpteenth time, I told Lakeesha that she couldn't bring her dog on the cable cars anymore. "But *he's* blind!" she told me. "I can't leave him alone when I'm out cleaning." So now not only was she "blind," the dog was "blind" too. Give me a break.

"It *will* be blind if I catch it," I said, not exactly cool.

"Oh, leave her be," an old white coot in a nearby seat told me.

"Just following the rules, sir," I spat.

Then I didn't see Lakeesha the cleaning lady for a couple of weeks. When I finally did, she didn't look good. I hesitated about checking her handbag for the pooch. Then I thought, Damn it. If I can't have a pet rat, then she can't have a pet dog! "Lakeesha, let me inspect your handbag!" It was my conductor's job, but this one couldn't be bothered, either.

"No!" Lakeesha said.

"We'll see about that," I replied. I swung around and grabbed the handbag and pulled it open. There was nothing inside but a couple of tissues and some rouge in a compact.

"See," Lakeesha said.

"What did you do, leave him at home today?"

Lakeesha looked down. "I don't have Barker any longer," she said.

"But how will you be able to see without him?" I spat.

"I'll get by," she said. She looked away.

"Did little Barker die?" I finally asked.

"Not yet. He has maybe three days, I think."

"What?"

"I had to take him to the pound. I couldn't afford him no more."

"Oh, my God."

"You won't have to search my handbag ever again."

"Well, good!" I said.

Yeah, yeah, yeah, you're right. I was a complete and total asshole.

Soon after that, I didn't see Lakeesha anymore, either. I think she died of a broken heart. God, the lives people lead!

ଔ ଓ

Today is New Year's Day. Yay! Actually this is my least favorite day of the year, technically I refer to New Year's Eve – all that fake frivolity and camaraderie, to say nothing of the still-drunk and hung-over on my cable cars this morning! Puleeze! I don't drink, at least not any more. Not since I burned a hole in my bedclothes and almost burned to death. That was four years ago. So, lucky me, I get to work on New Year's and face the gloom and cold and the post-partiers cold, stone sober.

So it was doubly nice when Darlene, my "girlfriend," came by my route and joined me on my car today.

I think she was trying to make up for being a pill since I had her carted off to the emergency room. She didn't say anything about that and tried to hold my hand. Tried to. I told her it wasn't safe. She looked a little disappointed, but, hey, I'm not "easy." Just hold her hand and I forgive and forget how distant she's been? I don't think so!

Darlene was looking pretty good today, though, I have to admit, for a fifty-eight-year-old. Even for a forty-eight-year-old. I believe she was wearing some new "regenerating" lotion below her eyes, and she hinted at some laser treatment she'd had done on her forehead.

"You mean Botox?" I asked.

"It's more up-to-date than that," she said, all high and mighty. "Do you like my new outfit?" She stood up and showed off this green and gold pants suit.

"It's great!" I enthused. Actually, it made her look like an elf. She was carrying a gift-wrapped box, which I was sure contained sugar cookies, her favorite. "What's in the box?" I asked.

"None of your business," she said.

"Okay." I shrugged.

"You have to earn what's in the box."

"I'm trying to lose weight."

She shrugged.

"So glad you came to visit me today," I said, lamely.

Darlene sat there as if deciding whether to leave or not. "Can I ring your bell?" she said, standing and pointing to the cord to the cable car bell above our heads.

"We're not supposed to use it too much," I answered.

"What do you mean? You ring it all the time."

"Not anymore, we don't. Just once in a while." It wasn't the truth.

"Oh, for God's sake, why do you make everything so difficult?!" Darlene snapped.

"We use the bells only for emergencies. MUNI's cracking down."

"Well, has it ever crossed your mind that maybe we're having an emergency?!"

"And you think ringing the cable car bell is gonna help?" I said.

"It could."

"Why? . . . Because I don't think so."

"Oh, you!" She sat down with her arms crossed over her chest and sulked. "You don't even know how to let a person be nice to you!"

"This is being nice?"

"I'm going to get off at the next stop."

I was expected to say, "No, darling Darlene, I can't let you go! Come here and ring my bell!" Only I didn't.

She looked perturbed. "You're not going to say anything?"

"What should I say?"

"Oh, forget it!"

"Okay, I've forgotten."

"I really am going to get off at the next stop." She looked at me with her best threatening stare.

"I guess I can't stop you from getting off if you insist, Miss!" I said.

We both stood there silent for a while. I knew that if I didn't say something right away, and just the way she wanted me to say it, Darlene might very well get off the cable car and we'd never speak again, let alone have sex. However, I wasn't sure I wanted the two of us to go on, even with sex.

"Alright then," Darlene said, getting up. The next stop was about a hundred yards away. "Have a happy new year – by yourself."

Before I could find my tongue she had descended the steps on the cable car and was in the street, hurrying off. I noticed that she had left her box of sugar cookies behind on the seat. I picked it up and was going to throw it after her. I even muttered, "I don't want your damn fattening cookies, bitch!" and held the box up with one hand.

Then I felt something moving inside the box. What the hell? I thought. When I opened it, there were no loose cookies or dancing gingerbread men or anything else to eat. There was a white rat with a pink ribbon around its neck staring up at me, half terrified, half curious. Oh Christ, Darlene had brought me a new pet, to replace Bitty and had even tied a ribbon around its neck – for me – and she hated rats!

I replaced the lid on the box quickly, even though there were no air holes, to be sure my gift didn't escape and then looked for Darlene, but she was out of sight by then.

When I called later on my break she didn't answer. I called fifteen times.

I ate Bitty the Second for lunch.

NO!!! I didn't!!!

I am thinking about turning him over to the SPCA – or maybe training him to hide inside my MUNI jacket . . . But I don't know if I can stand another lost pet. I know I should call Darlene and thank her for the gift. I know it, but I haven't done it. I can't decide whether I want Darlene or not.

CR 80

Why is it so difficult maintaining a relationship with my girl?! I'm a nice guy. Darlene's a nice gal. We're both mature, have been through the mill, both understand people (me a little bit better than she does because I deal with the public more). It's not like either of us has umpteen other choices, either! And yet there is this constant friction, bordering on annoyance. Over the border a lot of the time! Could it be the friction keeps the interest alive? I've seen plenty of happier couples who have nothing to say to each other anymore, except shit like "How's your frozen yoghurt?"

At least Darlene and I are alive. She yelled at me on the phone for fourteen and a half minutes today, about the way I handled her present of the pet rat. "It almost gave me rabies!" she screamed. It didn't. I also didn't say, "So you gave me a gift with rabies?" Anyhoo, we "talked," but we both agreed to give "us" a break for a while.

Did I ever tell you the story about Darlene and the chocolate muffin? Now this is a true story, I swear on my sainted mother's head! My mother was not all that sainted, but that's another story.

The story about Darlene's chocolate muffin is as follows:

Every Valentine's Day Darlene got this old chocolate muffin out of a storage bin in her kitchen. She'd had it since she was a child, given to her by her grandmother from Alsace-Lorraine, or some such. Darlene had taken one little bite out of it when she first got it, then wrapped up the rest and was "saving it for a rainy day," the way she had been taught. The days came and went, some of them pretty rainy too, but Darlene never ate the remainder of the chocolate muffin. The muffin was so old it had gone through several stages. First it crumbled. Then what was left hardened. Over time it had become not only inedible but unbreakable. Even the cockroaches in Darlene's kitchen couldn't make a dent in it, and, believe me, those suckers tried. (Peace, Darlene!)

One day last year Darlene decided to throw away the rock-like old muffin and wanted me to go with her to throw it in sight of the Bay Bridge. "It will be like me accepting my mortality," she said rather ominously. "Can't you just put it in the garbage?" I said, quite reasonably, it seemed to me. Still, Darlene insisted that we go by cable car all the way from Powell and Market to the Embarcadero.

But we didn't get that far, only half way.

It just happened to be Valentine's Day, and a sunny one at that. There were tons of tourists on the cable car. It was my day off, but I knew Stan, the conductor that day, and since I worked for MUNI he let us both ride for free. He's a prick in most other ways, but he did stretch company policy, and a good thing for him it was too! You see, as we started climbing up to Nob Hill, I heard a creak or a crack. That's not good, I told myself. It sounded like the underground cable itself might have developed a glitch. Or it could have been one of the hooks (the grabbers) on the car itself that was not working properly.

The cable car stopped, and we all were jerked forward, not enough to injure anyone, but disconcerting, shall we say. Grover, the gripman, put on the emergency brake and jumped off to survey the problem. I decided that I had better check it out as well. Stan stayed on and tried to assure the passengers that everything was fine.

Darlene got down off the car with me. Just then, the cable car lurched, and a collective cry went up from the passengers. "*Gott im Himmel. Ve* are doomed!" somebody yelled.

I didn't contradict Adolph What's His Name. The mechanics of the cable cars, if you want my unvarnished opinion, are not that good. In fact, they are TERRIBLE. But they are such a sacred cow nobody can point out the obvious: The cable cars are OLD and UNSAFE.

Suddenly there was another squeal from the tracks under our cable car. Stan, Grover, and I each got down on one knee and looked underneath. It was hard to see, to be honest. There was another creaking noise, and I thought there go about thirty people to their tourist deaths, slamming into who knew how many cars and buses and pedestrians – and panhandlers – before coming to a fiery stop at the bottom of the hill.

I hadn't counted on Darlene and her diamond-hard chocolate muffin from her grandmother from Alsace-Lorraine. Silly me.

Darlene pulled the black object out of the storage bin that she was carrying and stuffed it into the left-side track, just behind the cable car. She fiddled with it and tamped it down with her fist, causing a big bruise later. But that muffin held, and all the tourists were saved on that Valentine's Day, until the regular repair crew could get out and get us on the road again. Darlene did not even have to throw away the aged chocolate muffin. It had disintegrated into tiny bits as it saved all those lives as we climbed halfway to the stars.

And if you believe that story, you deserve to be conned by Jamaicans!

03 80

Skip this next story. It's not very nice.

Yet I am committed to telling stories that "illuminate life, as I experience it," not crap. There is more money in crap, of course, but I don't want to sell it. I think it's bad for people. Considering how full of shit most people are, both metaphorically and literally, you'd think they would want less crap coming into their souls. So think of me as a purgative. I used to think folks wanted to see the truth in things, but I have come to realize they really do not. So be it. So six people read these tales. That's fine with me. I will not hand out spiritual pornography! Who was it that said, "I don't care if this movie makes a dime, just as long as every man, woman, and child in America sees it"?! I'll be happy if I get a couple of nods in agreement. Now there's the Triumph of the Human Spirit!

There was this gentleman, broadly defined, who came onto my cable car a few days ago. He thought I didn't see it, because he was carrying it in a shopping bag, but of course I did. He had a machete in the bag, sticking out. He looked annoyed and sheepish at the same time. He looked vaguely bi-cultural, like those actors you see now in TV ads, now that the "demographics" have changed, meaning the invasion of one or several human species that don't look like me. God bless 'em, they are reproductive! I don't have any kids myself, except maybe that American Indian woman's, and it looks like it's going to stay that way.

Some other guy about forty who was sweating badly had just run up to my cable car and tried to get on, then changed his mind, and ran off up the hill. He looked like he was up to no good. But at least he was out of my hair now. Good riddance.

I wondered if I should confront Machete Man or just let him be. Plenty of weapons are smuggled onto the cable cars and all the other modes of transportation in San Francisco. We simply look away if in doubt and hope for the best.

"How are you doing, sir?" I finally said to Machete Man.

He knew that I knew. "Just fine. And you?"

"Fine."

We rode along for a few seconds as I pondered whether to make him get off. He was a big guy. I knew I might be taking my life into my own hands. We aren't allowed to pack a weapon while we're working. I'm not a big gun freak, but there are times when I think I'm at an unfair disadvantage. I'm not for guns – except for me!

"Did you hear what happened?" Machete Man suddenly asked me.

"What do you mean?"

"Some fucker from the Tenderloin was seen running toward a cable car about half an hour ago."

"Yeah?" It sounded like it could have been the sweating guy I'd seen.

"He killed this woman's little dog."

"What?!"

"She doesn't live in the Tenderloin like I do, but she had stopped her car and got out to get her phone from under the passenger seat, trying to obey the law. This dude sees her talking on her cell phone and comes up to her and says, "Give me your money." She got startled, naturally, and didn't understand what he was saying to her. He was this big, mumbly voiced dude about forty. He grabs her cell phone and is about to run away with it when he notices some loose cash in that compartment between the driver's seat and the passenger's seat, about a hundred dollars. He tells the woman to give it to him, and she leans in to get it, but apparently she isn't fast enough for him, so he pushes her to the side and reaches through the open window, to grab the cash. In the back seat there is this little mixed Pekingese / Pug dog that she had rescued from the pound last year. It starts barking at the thief, and the dude says to the woman as he waves the cash he's stealing right in her face, "And I'm gonna kill your fucking dog too!" Then he actually leaned further in and grabbed the dog and threw it into oncoming traffic. It was immediately run over and started squealing. The woman tried to get her dog and managed to do so, but it died in her arms. She was covered with its blood. The dude just laughs and says, "I told you I'd do it" and walks away.

"That's hideous," I said. I wasn't even thinking about my own pet rat, Bitty the First. It was hideous all on its own.

"So have you seen this dude by any chance?" Machete Man asked me.

"What are you planning to do to him?"

"I just want to give him a piece of my mind." He touched the handle of the machete.

"Maybe the guy has problems."

"He's a total bag of shit."

"Are you sure you'd know him if you'd see him?"

"I spoke to the woman. She identified him. He was smelly and sweating all over the place. He must be sweating even more after running away."

"He could live somewhere around here, probably is back home now."

"I'll keep looking anyway," Machete Man said. He stiffened his back and sat back on his seat looking out toward the sidewalks. Some other passengers looked askance at him. I hemmed, I hawed.

As the cable car made its way up to the stars, I saw the sweating guy, now standing on a corner. He was even counting out the money he had stolen, although maybe I am misremembering that part. What I did not misremember is saying to Machete Man, "There he is, over there." I even pointed.

Machete Man's eyes met mine as he turned around, but neither of us smiled. He got off the car as soon as he could and started walking downhill toward Sweating Man. I did not look to see what happened next. In fact I looked away.

The next day I heard that some dude was found decapitated in some alley off Leavenworth. . . What a goddamned pity.

 CB ♌

Did I tell you I saw Harvey Milk on my cable car yesterday? In case you don't know, Harvey Milk was the first open cocksucker ever elected in San Francisco, back in the late 1970s. He and the mayor were assassinated by a disgruntled city Supervisor asshole. To be precise, I saw the ghost of Harvey Milk.

This Harvey was shadowy, as ghosts tend to be, a masculine man, not all that handsome, to be truthful, but he had a certain charisma even if he wasn't "all there." I don't believe in ghosts, so I was not afraid to speak to him. "How's it hanging, Harvey?" I said. I like to think I'm quite the kidder.

"I'm on my way to work," he replied.

"Really? What for?"

"I'm on the Board of Supervisors."

I hesitated. The man didn't seem to know he was a ghost. "What day do you think it is?" I asked.

"November 27."

"And what year?"

"1978, of course."

That's the day he and the mayor were shot to death in their offices. "I think maybe you should take the day off, Harvey," I said.

"What? Why?"

"It's not 1978."

"Sure it is."

I pointed at the other passengers, to call attention to their more modern clothes. "Look at them," I said.

"Yeah?"

"Don't their clothes, their hairstyles look different to you?"

"It's San Francisco!" He smiled.

I shook my head.

"Are you trying to tell me something?" Harvey said.

I didn't answer right away.

"Well, I have to get off here," he said. "I like to ride the cable cars and then walk over to City Hall. It's great exercise."

"I would not go in today if I were you," I finally said.

"What do you know that I don't know?" He lingered on the step as we stopped. "Huh? What?"

"Nothing," I said. I let him go without another word, not even a warning. I figured that Harvey Milk as a cock-sucking martyr was a thousand times more valuable to his cause than as just some bureaucrat working over at City Hall.

Somebody on the cable cars told me that they came to San Francisco to live because they read Armistead Maupin's *Tales of the City*. How naïve! If that mushy, touchy, feely San Francisco ever existed, which I doubt, it was so far in the past as to be as relevant as ancient Carthage. Carthage is ancient, right? San Francisco right now is a much tougher place. I see people competing with each other, struggling for turf: jobs, places to live more than I see group-hugs. Diversity is WAY over-rated as a way to live. It might be colorful, but so was the Tower of Babel. Even when they speak the same language, people want their own; it's much worse when you don't even know what others are saying to you.

Take, for instance, what happened to me not that long ago. This Hispanic cleaning lady – let's call her Teresa, because that's her name! – asked me if I needed my "*casa*" cleaned. I think she over-heard me talking to my conductor about what a mess my place is. I don't quite have that so-called "hoarding syndrome," but I am somewhat of a slob. I save old computer magazines, old flyers from Best Buy as well as Bed, Bath, and Beyoncé (or whatever it's called).

God, I even keep old political mailers! Judge What the Fuck is for JUSTICE! That kind of thing. I can't seem to throw anything away.

So, anyhow, this Teresa says to me, "I good. Not from Mexico!" She seemed to think that was a recommendation of some kind.

"Where are you from?" I asked her.

"Guatemala."

"How much do you charge?"

"Thirty buck an hour."

"Thirty dollars an hour!? That's too rich for my blood."

She looked me up and down. She had these penetrating black, black eyes. Her eyebrows were on the ample side, not quite growing into one brow but close enough. She was short, busty, and wearing pink lipstick. "For you I clean for less," she informed me. "Once a week. *Si*?" She had even less charm than I do!

"How about two hours every two weeks?"

"*Que*?"

"Less."

"Twenty-five buck for hour?"

"I don't think I can afford that," I said.

"Two hours thirty buck?"

"How often? How long?"

"You say!"

"Every two weeks?"

"*Si.*"

So we agreed, I thought, to her cleaning my condo two hours every other week for thirty dollars each time? Right?

She came over to my place two days later, and I gave her a trial. She ran the vacuum sweeper, mopped the kitchen floor, cleaned out Bitty the Second's litter bin, and moved some of my medications around so that they were hard to find – all in all not a bad first cleaning. I thank her profusely and handed her a check for thirty dollars.

"The cash! The cash!" she insisted.

"I don't have cash. Can't you take a check?"

"No check! No check!" She waved her arms around. "No taxes! No taxes!"

I scrounged around and found twenty seven dollars in an old, empty paprika box that I use to hide money. I hid it from Teresa of Guatemala. So I'm a racist because I don't want to get ripped off??!! Fuck you. I am nobody's sucker.

"I will give you the rest when you return," I said carefully with lots of money gestures.

Teresa seemed happy with the arrangements.

So why am I telling you this? Because yesterday when I came home, expecting to find my place cleaned up and after trusting that woman with a key, where is she? Cleaning? Hardly. She was in my bed, naked, except for the pink lipstick. "Thirty buck. *Si*?" she said. "For two hours?"

I can't go for two hours! Who can go for two hours? We're both lucky if Darlene and I go for seven minutes! Jesus, I'm not Casanova!

No, I did not jump into bed with Teresa of Guatemala. She pouted and I protested. She threatened to leave and I offered her forty dollars for an hour and half of *cleaning* every other week. She doesn't do windows, but she does mop a mean kitchen and restacks my Bed, Bath, and Beyond coupon flyers like a pro. We rarely speak when she's there, but it's probably best that way. Now who is exploiting who, I ask you?

Cؠؠ ؠؠ

There are plenty of pretty gals on the cable cars, believe you me. And quite a few of them seem to like me. Not that I'm bragging. It must be the uniform. Who can resist a brown uniform? Not that I take advantage of my position. I'm in a Committed Relationship with Darlene, wherever the hell she is. I have not seen her for over month. Maybe she's a Missing Person! . . . You think? Maybe she ran off with the postman. I always suspected Darlene has a thing for uniforms too.

I know better than to ask passengers out. It may even be in my job description. No sexual harassment of passengers. It's really hard these days to know where the line is. In the old days, you could ask a lady if she wanted to go out on a date. Now you have to wait until she practically grabs your crotch before you can say boo. I liked the old days better. Of course in the old days, women didn't put out as much either. So whatcha gonna do?! Fuck AIDS!

But I gotta tell you I was really tempted today. This stunning woman with auburn hair and a tight green sweater got on near the Westin San Francisco at Post and caught my eye almost immediately. She was wearing this very subtle make-up, making her look very attractive, not slutty, the way so many of the younger gals do these days, all painted up. I made eye contact with the beauty and tipped my invisible cap to her. She came over and sat right beside me. I barely had to turn my head in order to talk to her.

"You visiting?" I asked.

"No, I live there, at the St. Francis."

"You do?" I thought that must be pretty pricey but didn't voice the words.

"My father owns it," she said.

I turned my head completely. "Your father owns the St. Francis Hotel?"

"He does."

"I thought the Westin Corporation, or whatever it's called, owned it."

"He's one of the financial partners."

"Well, that must be nice," I said lamely. I figured she must be a Republican. Well, I'm a Republican, but only on Tuesdays and Fridays.

"Not too shabby." She grinned.

There was a lull, and I let down my half of the conversation.

"Business has been a little off this year," she volunteered.

She wants me! I thought. Maybe some kind of Lady Chatterley's Lover trip: The Heiress and the

Cable Car Gripman. Maybe she wanted me to talk dirty to her in cable car slang!? I'd like to couple with your caboose – that kind of thing, only better. (I'm not telling you our secret cable car lingo, kiddo.)

I figured the heiress was around forty, a very well preserved forty, but you can still tell that she was no spring chicken. I'm 52, so the age spread wasn't that bad. I bet she'd like to be spread-eagled on one of her Posturepedic mattresses at the St. Francis! I thought, getting myself all hot and bothered. Would she expect me to pay for the room, or would it be her treat? Did they still expect you to sign in as husband and wife, or was I showing my age? Would they recognize the heiress at the front desk and say, "Welcome back, Miss Westin." Yeah, maybe she did this all the time. Was she a nymphomaniac maybe? Hot damn! One could hope.

I looked over again. "Funny, I haven't seen you on the cable cars before," I said.

"I've been living in New York."

"Here's better."

"In some ways," she agreed. "Not in all ways."

"Better weather," I ventured. Jeez, I'm talking about the weather with this babe who wants my body!

"You do have nice year-round weather," the heiress said. "Are you married with kids?" she went on.

121

"No, single." (Shut up, Darlene. Answer your phone!)

"I recently divorced." There was a wistful tone to her words.

"Sorry to hear that." Yeah, sympathize. Women like that.

"He became a jerk, over time."

"Yeah, some men can be jerks." I nodded. "Not all of us, though!"

"It's not easy meeting men in San Francisco," she said. "They're all gay."

"Not all of us." I turned and smiled my biggest smile.

"I've tried those online dating services. A disaster."

"Really?"

"I dated three men. Not one of them looked like their picture. Not one!"

"Yeah, you want to know what you're getting." Was that the best thing to say?

"One of them asked if I was a round-heeled woman. Can you imagine?!"

"How awful! What nerve." I had no idea what a round-heeled woman was.

"Another one on the phone asked me how much I weighed."

"Well, I hope you didn't tell him," I said indignantly.

"I hung up on him."

"Good for you." Agree with her. Women like that. Darlene certainly does. "What was wrong with the third guy?"

"He had psoriasis. On his neck. And not just a little bit of it, either. Plus two tattoos of women's breasts on either side of his neck. I think he believed the tattoos would cover up or distract from his psoriasis. They didn't."

"Probably made it worse," I threw in.

"Absolutely. And then he was indignant and called me a 'racist' because I wouldn't sleep with him."

"Dating's hard," I said.

"But I'm not going back to my ex-husband."

"Of course not."

"My father wants me to marry another one of the Westin partners, to keep the money together. But I want to play the field more. I was married at nineteen and had sex with just my husband during my whole life."

TMI? I thought. Oh, let her vent. Sounds like she's been through a lot even if she is rich. I'm smart enough to realize that wealthy folks have problems. Even some of those lottery winners wind up committing suicide!

"Are you seeing anyone?" the heiress asked me.

"I just broke up with my girlfriend."

"Are you sure?"

"Would I lie to a beautiful woman like you?" See, I can be snappy when I need to be.

"We could meet for coffee tomorrow at the Oak Room at the St. Francis," she said. "Do you work tomorrow?"

"For you I'd take off the whole day," I said. I was on a roll now!

"How about three o'clock? We'll have tea."

I got such a boner you wouldn't believe! "That sounds like a winner to me!" I gushed.

I looked back to make eye contact, and just then I saw Darlene standing on the sidewalk at Pine Street glaring at me. Was she planning to climb aboard? Did she have a gun? Did she want to make up? Did she just want to "talk"? Meaning Darlene laying down the law and jabbering without interruption for an hour!

"I'd love to meet for tea at the St. Francis," I told the heiress. "Do I have to get all dressed up?" "Wear your uniform. That way I'll recognize you.

Mostly I can only see the side of your head now." Wow! Maybe it really was the uniform.

"I'll be there." Luckily I was set to be off duty at two anyway.

I drove right past Darlene, even though she moved up. I pretended not to see her. Then she waved, but too late.

The heiress got up to get off at the next stop and brushed her hand across the hair on the nape of my neck. "It was very nice chatting with you," she said. "I'm looking forward to our tea tomorrow."

"Two for tea," I said, turning quite giddy, even though I was trying to be cool.

"It's just tea, remember," the heiress said, giving my hair a little slap.

Then as she stepped off the cable car step, I opened my big trap and the words shot out, "Then I'm gonna fuck your rich-bitch piece of ass until you see stars!"

The heiress turned back and looked at me as if she couldn't believe her ears. Such a scowl fell over her face as I haven't seen since Sister Mary Agatha in third grade. "What?!" she said. "*What?!*"

She stepped into the street, put her head down, and just kept walking with her shoulders hunched.

"I . . . I . . ." I stammered.

No, I didn't go to the tea. I figured the uniform maybe wouldn't be enough.

03 80

Generally I sympathize with people's sexual problems. I think most do not get much sex, not nearly as much as they need. What's all this nonsense about "sex addicts"?! Most straight men get about a minute of sex every Xmas! Big whoop. No wonder they go berserk and kill other people. (Are you listening, Darlene?)

But there is this creepy guy who rides the cable cars sometimes that I cannot seem to find any sympathy for. His name is Jimbo Saccarini, or something like that. He is about 6' 3" with a face like a gorilla's, only not as attractive as that. I think he is around fifty and has really bad legs. He hobbles. I think I overheard him say once that he has had both knees replaced. Too bad you can't have a soul replacement.

Did I mention that Jimbo is quite funny? I think he works as a stand-up comedian at various comedy clubs around town. He can even make fun of himself at times. He said some woman came up to him once and pushed cookie dough all over his face. "She wanted to make gorilla cookies," he said, deadpan. It was right on the mark.

I've talked to this guy privately at various times and he's alright. He can have a one-on-one conversation and even listen. But if there is even more person involved in the conversation, Jimbo goes into Performance Mode and turns into this smart-ass, mean son-of-a-bitch "comedian." He could have just been commiserating with you about your girlfriend (let's call her Darlene, for instance), and then all of a sudden Jimbo is telling the other passengers stuff like "Darlene's this guy's girlfriend. She's fifty-eight going on ninety-two! He met her in an old folks' home, or was it the morgue?" He'll turn to his victim and try to get you to join in on your own ridicule. If even one person half-laughs, he'll go on a riff for minutes at a time. He practices his "jokes" on people and keeps forgetting that he's told you the same joke seven times already. One day he even stopped this stammering kid who was trying to be funny too with "Shut up. You're not funny. I'm funny."

I think this Jimbo is gay. Now I really have nothing against gays. Remember I "dated" a man-nun twice, and other things here and there. So that makes me an Honorary Gay, I'd say. Still, Jimbo is sort of a major creep about it. He tries to pick up young men on the cable car and God knows where else, like bus terminals. I mean young men, maybe fourteen, fifteen, alone, arriving in the big city, naïve. He even tried to show me a picture of this teenager with a big hard-on, as if I wanted to see that! Jesus. He's not helping the gay cause, trust me.

I suppose Jimbo has a hard time finding love or even sex, because he is so unattractive. Did I mention that he's fat too? He gets on the cable car with a gallon of peppermint patty ice cream and he'll finish it before we get to his stop. "My mother was mean to me when I was a child," he says constantly. "I was born on the fifth, sixth, and seventh of August – I spent all that time dodging my mother's coat hanger!"

It's indeed a terrible thing if your own mother doesn't love you, or even like you, but I bet Jimbo was a difficult child. He is mouthy as an adult. I imagine he was as a child too. Just last week he told another passenger "Why don't you sit in the back, with the cripples. Excuse me, I mean the handicapped! With a face like yours, who wouldn't call you handicapped?!"

And this is from a man who himself can barely walk and has a face that can stop a train! Another passenger threatened to rip Jimbo a new one and even got up. But he was so unsteady he couldn't do much. "Sit down, Mike Tyson!" Jimbo spat. "Before I shit in your mouth. And I wouldn't want to do anything you'd like too much."

I don't know if I should report Jimbo as a public nuisance or not. Today he was trying to sidle up to this pimply-faced "youngin" who still had his suitcase with him. "I've always wanted to ride one of these cable cars!" the kid announced to everybody in his rural Arkansas accent.

"You must have just arrived," Jimbo said.

"I did, sir. I did."

"Do you have a job?"

"No, but I reckon I can find one soon enough."

"Don't be too sure," Jimbo said. "The market's tight, the way I was when I was your age!"

I don't think the kid got the joke.

"I need my apartment cleaned," Jimbo went on. "I'll give you twenty bucks and all you can eat."

The kid looked dubious.

"No pressure," Jimbo said. He was certainly taking a risk of being beaten up by these not exactly small "boys" from the backwoods.

"Where do you live?" the youngin enquired.

"Not too far. You can have your own bed."

"Well, I'd hope so!" Joe of Arkansas said. "What about your wife? Won't she object?"

"She's dead," Jimbo said. Actually he did actually have a wife, from Israel, whom he had married for money and because she needed a green card. The marriage was never consummated and she lived elsewhere, according to Jimbo.

"I'm sorry to hear that," Joe of Arkansas said.

"Yeah, I miss her like mad," Jimbo said.

I wanted to speak out to both of them. This rendezvous did not look promising for either party.

"I'd better call my momma and tell her I've arrived."

"You do that. You want to use my call phone?" Jimbo got his smart phone out and offered it.

"You'd do that for me?"

"A boy needs to talk to his momma. My momma never talked to me, not once!"

"Really?"

"Well, if she did, she said hateful things, like "You ruptured my spleen when you took your own good time climbing out of my hole!"

"Your momma said that?" Joe of Arkansas sat back, still holding his suitcase on his lap, and examined Jimbo's face, which had assumed a Sad Look.

"Yeah, she damaged me. I was perfect before I was born."

Joe of Arkansas looked over toward me as if for some message. Was Jimbo a serial murderer perhaps? Was it safe going to his apartment?

I didn't know what to do exactly. The kid looked like he might be eighteen.

"Here's the twenty dollars upfront," Jimbo said, taking two tens out of his wallet.

"I don't know about that." Joe of Arkansas twisted his youngin lips into a kind of knot.

"You afraid to clean for a living?" Jimbo said. "I have a hard time cleaning my place. I can barely get around." He pointed to his knees. "It would be a big help."

"Your knees, huh?" Joe of Arkansas giggled a little. "You ought to keep off them knees."

Jimbo looked at me and almost winked. He seemed to be saying, "See, this kid knows the score. To the boy he said in a fake Arkansas accent, "Now I hope you all wouldn't try to exploit a crippled old man with thee ar-thi-ritis, now would ya, boy?"

"Exploit? That's a big word."

"I can teach you lots of big words, son."

"I think my momma warned me about folks like you."

"My momma can beat up your momma!" Jimbo said, riffing.

"Have you met many fellas like me on this here cable car?" Joe asked.

"You're my very first," Jimbo said. "I swear on my momma's vagina!"

"You talk dirty!" Joe of Arkansas said.

"You ain't heard nothin' yet, kiddo."

"I don't know. Maybe I ought to get me over to the YMCA."

"Oh, you're gay?" Jimbo said.

"I ain't gay!" Joe of Arkansas said. "I'm a Christian!"

Jimbo looked my way and said, "Did I ever tell you what foreplay means? Two hours of me begging!" He snorted.

"I turned around and said to the newcomer, "You'd better go to the YMCA, kid."

"Thanks a lot," Jimbo spat.

"Don't take advantage," I said.

"Who do you think will take more advantage, me or him?"

"He seems pretty innocent."

"Yeah, right. They learn fast enough. Trust me."

"Do you want me to get the police involved?" I said.

"Yeah, report the hideous agony of getting a blow job!" Jimbo got up on his bad knees and started to leave the cable car. "You don't seem to understand how hard I have to work for a goddamned orgasm!"

"Try someone a little older," I said.

"Well, I don't like fifty-five-year-old pussy! Fuck you!" Poor old Jimbo was walking fast, rocking from side to side.

"Good riddance," I managed.

Suddenly Joe of Arkansas was standing up as well, catching up to Jimbo. "Is this our stop?"

"It will do," Jimbo said, smiling over at me. "We can catch a cab from here."

Joe of Arkansas turned toward me. "I really, really enjoyed my very first cable car ride! Thank you very, very much, sir!"

"Just doing my job," I answered.

The two of them got off, bad knees, suitcase, and all.

I saw Jimbo again about a month later. "What happened to that kid with the suitcase?" I asked.

"He wouldn't leave my dick alone. It's still got a rash on it. I thought he'd never leave. God!" Jimbo complained.

"Your momma would be proud of you," I snarked.

"You didn't know my mother, not for one second. She was a terrible, terrible mother. So shut up!"

Yep, Jimbo's mother no doubt had to deal with a terrible, terrible child. How do I know? . . . Because he still *was*.

CB BO

Lest you call me anti-gay because of my last little tale, as if one story is all a man thinks about a topic, let me tell you about the wedding that took place on my cable car between two lesbians. This was back during the short time that California permitted gay marriages, before the Good Citizens passed Proposition 8 to ban it. (Hello, Latinos and blacks!) I wasn't the one who performed the marriage ceremony, but I probably would have if I'd been asked, if I had a legal right to do so, and if I wasn't so busy steering the wedding venue!

The minister was some nondescript little Asian official from City Hall, I'd guess. He didn't look all that comfortable, but he was doing his duty, at least as defined at the time. The bride – were they two brides or two grooms? I'm not being a smartass. I've seen plenty of butch / femme lesbian couples in my day, but these two both seemed sort of in-between, like Ellen what's her name, that TV lesbian, the nice one, not Rosie O'Donnell, the brash, snippy one. Remember Rosie on the steps of City Hall bragging about how Out she was, how wonderful her gay marriage was going to be? And then in no time she goes and gets a divorce! It was probably her partner's decision to Get Out. Rosie O'Donnell must be hell to live with.

Anyway, here were these two women in their early thirties getting married on my cable car. One was wiry and almost pretty, wearing a muffler around her neck because it was a bit blustery that day. The other woman was fuller-bodied, with a noticeable gap between her teeth, wearing glasses. Neither was going to be Miss America, you might say, but they were no uglier than most people. Most people are pretty ugly, or at least plain. No wonder we prize beauty so much. They both seemed to be ecstatic to be getting married. I don't think gays really care that much about the actual marriage, do they? Are the tax breaks that terrific? Do you really want to mix up your bank accounts with somebody else's? I wouldn't trust Darlene with mine! It's really about social acceptance, isn't it? To be honest, I've always found it rather odd that anybody wants to get up in front of a bunch of other people and declare their Legal Right to Fuck. Go ahead and fuck without a ceremony. I don't care. Just don't scare the cable cars!

With the couple were their two kids, a boy with reddish hair, about six, and a tiny girl about four. I think each woman was a mother. The kids looked just like them, only cuter.

The Lesbian Wedding Ceremony took place near the rear of the cable car. Johan, the conductor that morning, rang the cable car bell too many times to signal the start. I think he was over-compensating because underneath it all he didn't really approve of same-sex marriage (or same-sex anything, except maybe football!) A few friends of the couple were on board and beamed like drunken Gospel singers as the ceremony began in earnest. "You go, girl!" and "Hallelujah!" rang out more than once. I couldn't hear all the words, but I think "obey" was omitted from the vows. You're not making those gals obey no patriarchal mother-fuckers' rules, trust you me! The little official did say something about "commitment" and "endless cunnilingus." But I could be mistaken about the cunnilingus. (I'd sign up for endless cunnilingus if I could get it!) There was a kiss, a chaste one on the lips, and a big hug.

I didn't tear up, but an old lady who just happened to be on the cable car at that moment did so.

The lesbian in the muffler asked the official if she could say a few words. She said, "Irene, you have made me complete. I was so miserable until I met you. May we live as a couple until the end of time!" Ahhh. The one with the gap between her teeth said, "Marsha Jean, I love you very much. You make me less selfish every day. You keep my heart free of bitterness. And I will stay with you through thick and thin, and we will never, never part." Double Ahhh. Yeah, it was a bit excessive in those promises. The best marriages don't last "until the end of time," no matter what the songs say. And unless they both happen to die simultaneously, there is a very strong possibility that they will part, no matter how much they may not want to. And I also think there's something called Lesbian Bed Death that sets in after a few years of nesting together. Whatever! It was a happy occasion, and I wasn't going to spoil it by butting in with my observations. And if you think I'm grumpy, read some of those old fart Supreme Court justices! Of course now that I have seen a gay wedding, I was desperately to marry a goat!

No hordes of evangelicals boarded the cable car and pulled the lesbians to pieces. The Pope did not ride by in his Pope-mobile and throw burning incense at them. Even the folks who had voted for Proposition 8 (and you know who you were!) on that day pretended to be pleased with the Sodom and Gomorrah right there in front of them on that cable car and applauded as the ceremony came to its end. I even heard one other little girl say, "Mommy, where do lesbians come from?" "From Heaven, honey" was the answer. AHHHH!!!!

As the wedding party departed, one of the new married couple said to everyone, "Now we can get busy on that new baby!" Everybody applauded that as well. (Hmm, now we have to worry about the gays contributing to the goddamn population explosion?!)

ᓚ ᕽ

It's crazy how on one day two lesbians can be declaring their Lesbian Love and even getting hitched on my cable car and the next day somebody gets punished for virtually the same thing. It just goes to show that having all our Blessed Diversity is hardly always a good thing for certain people.

Take, for exactly, Felicity, am effeminate youth from Chinatown who used to ride with me a couple of times a week. We go right through Chinatown, which is "colorful" but also rather ugly, if you look at it without rose-colored, tourist eyes. I went to Hong Kong once, and it was the same there: overcrowded and crummy-looking. The people looked clean and well-dressed, but their shops sure didn't. Don't tell me what I'm supposed to see and what I do see! Jesus! I'm not your goddamned publicity department!

Felicity Lieu was actually Felix Lieu, according to his birth certificate. I've never seen his birth certificate, but I saw him before he was "Felicity," a slender, almond-eyed young man of considerable grace and poise, with undulant arms. Is "undulant" a word? Is "almond-eyed" okay these days? He was always impeccably dressed in clothes that bordered on the "femme" side, shall we say. He wore his chestnut brown hair long and with a red highlight or two, here and there. If he wasn't already pretty, he enhanced very well, if you asked me. And then somewhere in there Felix had the Full Non-Monty and became Felicity. He even mentioned it to me when I gave him a double look the first time he boarded my car. "Yes, it is me," she said.

"Well, good for you," I responded, like a good P.C. San Franciscan. "I'm sure you are much happier now in your new body." Secretly I thought: I just hoped the city's health service didn't have to pay for it!

"Yes, it's much better now," Felicity said. "Only it's not perfect."

"Oh?" I said.

"I think I still look too mannish."

"You could fool me!" I snapped.

Felicity touched her delicate hand to her throat. "My Adam's apple."

"I can barely see it," I assured her.

"Oh, so you can see it?" She looked upset.

"Only to the trained eye!" I bragged.

"Oh my, I guess I will have to wear high necks all the time."

I thought, considering that this guy had given up his PENIS, high necks were a small price to pay! "Is this your first day out?" I asked.

"My first on a cable car."

I looked around. Nobody appeared to be staring at Felicity. She was "passing" just fine. "You look splendid," I said. "Good luck on your new venture!"

"I'm going shopping for more clothes."

"Well, you'll have lots to choose from. There is always more women's stuff than men's." I don't know why I said that, except that it was true, and Darlene was always saying how men had so much more in the world than women did. Not when it came to wearing apparel!

"Let me know how things go with you," I said as she got up for her stop. I actually was curious about how her life would change. Were women treated worse than men, even in America? Were they treated better? From my own observations, I saw that women often used their looks or their "helplessness" when it suited them, like with heavy luggage or the best seat on the cable car, and other things. They wanted it both ways, all the rights of men, all the perks of women. But was it worth the perks of women to give up your PENIS?! Or even, according to the Discovery Channel, splitting it and making it into your clitoris!? Please, God, not that!

I saw Felicity one or two more times after that first time. She was always wearing high collars. I think some of the high collars drew more attention than the Adam's apple would have. You had to give Felix Lieu credit for changing his life circumstances. What bravery! What guts!

Then I heard that his Old World parents found out about their son and invited him back home for dim sum and then killed him. The whole family surrounded him and smothered him with pillows. It seems that they didn't kill him because he had become a transsexual but because now he was a girl and they had missed him the first time around.

೫ ೮

Despite the fact that I see lots of people five days a week on my cable cars, I am somewhat lonely. It's not easy to admit, but it's true. Darlene has not come running back, the way I thought she would, and I am too stubborn to call her again. Maybe she's gone off and joined the Peace Corps. I checked her status on Facebook and she still has "in a relationship" posted, but maybe it's with somebody new. (She also doesn't keep her Facebook page up to date very well.)

Yeah, I exchange a few words with passengers, but they are not friends. The closest I have come to a "friend" is Darlene's brother, Sean, who works as a sous chef in the Marina. I don't see him very much, and now that I apparently am not seeing Darlene any longer, I don't see Sean at all. He's a bit obsessed with football and the Forty-niners, but he's good-natured and uncomplicated, and a relief to be around. He's a goof, and we all need a goof from time to time.

There is also this guy who rides the California line with me about once a week. His name is Joshua Epstein and I am beginning to think he may be anti-Gentile! Ever heard of one of those? How else to explain the fact that I rarely encounter him these days after what happened.

He was a serious, short, balding guy with really terrible skin, you know old acne craters and blotches that must have made his puberty a nightmare. He plays the clarinet almost like a pro. I've heard him at this restaurant/bar in the Fillmore, where he has a foursome that plays once in a while. He even had a special clarinet made in France or somewhere like that, for big bucks. But I'm not really a jazz fan, though I pretended for Joshua's sake. What I like about him is his conversation. He's a very sensitive listener, and he's straight! We've even had coffee a half dozen times at this spot on Post Street. You feel like you can tell him anything and he won't judge you. Our get-togethers were becoming sort of regular. Even his wife, Ruby, would come sometimes. She's pretty nifty too, but she doesn't listen as well as Joshua does. They even took me out for my 52nd birthday party several months ago. I just haven't heard from him since. Maybe it was a kiss goodbye, so to speak?

He's an herbalist by profession, "certified" according to him. I don't know what that means precisely. You can be a "certified herbalist"? Ain't San Francisco great?! I think it means he dropped out of medical school, but, hey, who am I to judge? I just went to college for one course. It just wasn't my cup of tea. Now I consider the cable cars my college, of Hard Knocks.

I started to feel that Joshua was pulling away from me when I said something positive about Israel, not that I really know that much about Israel – West Bank, Gaza Strip Joint, whatever. As I said, that ass won't wipe, if you ask me. You see, Joshua is one of those liberal Jews who are down on the Israelis and for the Palestinians, though what they see in those fuckers beats me. But I'm not "political." Who has the time?!

Then Joshua, even though he's stated numerous times that he is not religious and pretty much disavows his Jewish background, suddenly starts going to temple, or whatever you call it, and is studying the Torah, "from a secular point of view," according to Joshua. If you ask me, the whole Bible is a big bunch of baloney with far too many Thou Shalts in it for my taste, but if Joshua wanted to study the Torah, that was his business. Only then he started saying that he couldn't find time for our coffee get-togethers even once a week. It seems that he had signed up with his local temple and volunteered to help out. All of sudden he's running for president and working with his rabbi and he's elected and he's busy, busy, busy answering phone calls and dealing with "temple issues," and I don't have a talk buddy any longer. I've e-mailed him, gone to his jazz sessions, and left a couple of messages on his answering machines. But I don't hear back. If I do any more, he might think I want his body or something. I really don't. I just want somebody like him to talk to, that's all. I read an article one time that pointed out that most straight guys have almost no friends apart from their primary relationships, like their wives or maybe a relative. I always thought that was not true. But it is true, of me.

Boo hoo. I should shut up.

ভঃ ৪০

I got hold of Darlene on her cell phone today. She was sort of aloof. But we did manage to talk a bit. It was strained. "How were your holidays?" "How were yours?" — That kind of generic shit. From what I could figure out she spent the holidays drunk with her brother. I went to a movie at some big, cold "Cineplex" and snuck into two other movies for free.

And neither one of those movies was the least bit good! I like movies, but then they're over, and your life has to go on from there.

Darlene and I hung up without anything being resolved, not even getting together to "talk about us." I hate those kind of talks. Usually one or the other parties shows up with a gun! I wouldn't put shooting me past Darlene. She'd claim self-defense and have a well-thought-out explanation of why she had to shoot me! God, she's selfish! One of the last times I saw her she put on this Bob Dylan album much too loud, and I had to listen to fucking old Dylan's cracking, hollowed-out "singing"— devoid of anything approaching an actual singing voice. Darlene said, "You are tone deaf." But I think she's tone deaf if she thinks Bob Dylan can sing! So fuck Darlene and Bob Dylan! I'm not getting back together with her just because she's lonely!

I don't know what all this has to do with what I meant to tell you about, the movie star I saw on my cable car today. I am not going to name this star because I want you to guess. It was a woman, a woman of a "certain age," although she still looked terrific. She was really big years ago. She hasn't made a movie in ages, I'm pretty sure. No, it's not Tippy Hedrin. (Is that her name? Is it Tippi? What kind of a name is Tippi?) She's the one who starred in

Hitchcock's *The Birds*, right? What a dumb-ass movie that is. Those birds look so phony! And why in hell is Tippi or Trippi going up to the attic alone without a weapon when she knows for a fact that the BIRDS have pecked out some other dude's eyes!? And everybody's always going on and on about what a GENIUS Hitchcock was.

I don't get it.

Anyway, the star I saw today was not Tippi Hedrin. And it wasn't Kim Novak. Wasn't she the one is that other Hitchcock film, *Vertigo*? I saw that listed on some critics' list of The Greatest Movies of All Time! Really? The movie where they throw that obvious dummy out of the tower? Please! The greatest movie of all time is *Lassie Come Home*. No ifs, ands, or buts! I wish I could be nine years old again and cry like that!

Have you guessed who my movie star was yet? Maybe you won't remember her name, but she was BIG back in the day. Actually, she's gotten a bit big over the years. But she still looks really good.

Do you give up?

One more guess!

Okay, it was. . . Oh, God, what is her name? It was just on the tip of my brain a minute ago. Am I having a senior moment? For God's sake, I'm only fifty-two! My mother did suffer from Alzheimer's, though. I sure hope that is not my fate.

Fuck, what is her name!? I think it started with a V. Or maybe it was a W.

Okay, okay, I told you the cable cars take you just *half*way to the stars! Get it?!

ꞇ ꞇ

The governor of the Republic of Texas rode on my cable car today. He was here as part of the so-called "Texas Tornado Business Whirlwind" to lure away California businesses to his Great State. Why anyone would think that mentioning tornadoes would be an attraction of a place is for others to make sense of. But the Governor was not noted for his sensitivity to nuance, shall we say. I guess he just thought he might rassle up some San Francisco money any way he could. I just wish that he hadn't wanted to "ride me one of them cable car thingeys" while he was in town.

The Governor's name was Prick Rerry, or something along those lines, and he looked the part of an old-fashioned American president, chiseled nose, handsome granite jaw, steely blue eyes, salt-and-pepper pubic hair (to judge from his head hair), tall and sinewy, a very impressive physical specimen of manliness. Until he opened his yap, especially off the cuff. Then he was a PR director's nightmare.

The first thing he announced when he got on the cable car, to his four cohorts, but loud enough for everybody else to hear too, was: "These cable cars sure are small!" Passengers were whispering back and forth, trying to figure out who this well-dressed redneck might be.

"Don't worry, folks!" he said, holding up both hands. "I'm just on here as a tourist!" Nobody seemed to know who he was. At least they couldn't have cared less.

Luckily, the Governor wasn't my responsibility. He belonged to the conductor of the day, Ted Actouka, who is from Guam, I think. Ted is sort of odd-looking, with a small, very dark head and irregular features. He also loves to wear a lei around his neck sometimes. He isn't from Hawaii. He just likes leis. Anyway, he asked the Governor to have a seat for safety reasons. The Governor sees the lei and says "*Mahalo*, my friend!" But he refuses to sit down.

"I'm not from Hawaii," Ted Actouka says.

"I didn't say you was," the Governor answers back.

"You implied it," Ted Actouka answers him back. You could tell it was one of those situations where there is immediate anti-chemistry between people.

"No, your little flower-child necklace implied it, I'd say," the Governor says with a little more spite, still with a big wide Texan smile as phony as his capped teeth.

And it went downhill from there.

"You big blowhard!" Ted Actouka says.

"Come work in Texas!" the Governor says. "We'll build you a cable car that you can fit some people into!" He and his cohorts laughed. "And it won't creak along, neither!"

I turned around and gestured at Ted not to continue with this exchange.

He ignored me. Ted Actouka is very stubborn. "Why ride on a cable car if you want it to be different?" he almost shouts.

"I didn't want to ride on the damned thing in the first place. My staff thought it would be a nice gesture." The Governor's face was turning red underneath the deep tan. "I'm here to show that I'm not afraid of you all's 'San Francisco values.'" His little group of four cohorts applauded politely.

"I don't know what the hell 'San Francisco values" mean!" Ted Actouka shoots back. I know for a fact that Ted hates the Gay Parade and voted against same-sex marriage, so he is far from being a bleeding heart, if that's what the Governor meant. "You are just trying to steal our businesses! You hate unions!"

"I don't hate unions," the Governor answers. "I just don't want them to fuck me in the ass!"

"Oh, take your fucking tornadoes and get the hell back where you came from!"

"I'd better get home, before one of your earthquakes takes me to Jesus before my time!" The Governor was trying to sound like a cheery Good Ol' Boy, but he was not succeeding. "And just where are you from, friend? From the look of you, it must be a doozy!"

"It's better than Texas!" Ted Actouka snipes.

"Then it must be Heaven itself, 'cause nothin' is better on earth than Texas!"

"I hear Texas is nothin' but a great big asshole!"

"Well, since you're from San Francisco, or live here, you must know more about assholes than I ever would."

Passengers and cohorts were now all trying to calm down both men, not too well.

"Shut up! I'm not gay!" Ted Actouka defends himself. "A lei does not make me gay!" Now he was red in the face, not easy given his complexion. Well, at least Ted and the Governor agreed about the gays!

"You look gay to me!" the Governor counters. "I just didn't know gays came in so many different colors, like a rainbow!"

The cohorts were trying to outright shush the Governor by this time. They knew you couldn't even hint at "color" in a negative way in America.

"You don't like my color?" Ted Actouka says, jumping on what he knew to be his trump card. "And what color is that?" Ted asks. "Huh?"

"I love your color. I have a bird dog that looks just like you!"

"You are comparing me to a dog?"

"I love dogs!"

"You're a dog yourself!" Ted Actouka now starts going after the Governor. I wish I could say it was like an old cowboy movie with lots of fists and grown men falling onto chairs and the bar itself. But in this case they were actually slapping at each other. Ted landed a palm on the Governor's upper arm. The Governor landed a better one on Ted's irregular chin. They both hurt their hand more than the other guy.

"You son of a bitch hillbilly!" Ted Actouka says, wincing in pain.

"You goddamned girlie man hippie!" the Governor counters.

The funny thing was they both looked sort of "girlie" with all their slaps back and forth.

It ended as well as it could have, with the Governor's cohorts escorting him off the cable car as soon as they could get me to stop. Ted Actouka wound up with a sprained wrist. Oddly enough, nobody reported either party. I told Ted that I supported him over the Governor. But actually I thought they were both bigots. How dare Ted Actouka be so far behind the times about the gays, and how dare the fucking, idiotic Governor think he could come here and criticize my city! *I* can criticize San Francisco. But he can't. It's my San Francisco!

ᘓ ᘔ

And it's my America too!

What the fuck is happening to us!? Now we're having actual gun fights on the cable cars, not just little slapping hissy fits. We are one sick nation. And it seems to be everywhere.

Here in my town we have at least two Hispanic gangs going after each other. I don't know what their true names are. Let's call them the Bastardos and the Asshollas. They are notable for their ridiculous tattoos, creepy-crawly vines and skulls and other shit all the way up their necks, even some insects behind their ears. Their clothes are baggy and make them look even more over-weight than they are. They always have such Attitude written all over their faces you want to knock them back to where they came from, even if they were born here!

Lucky for me I was on a cable car behind the two where the gun fight took place yesterday. Two cable lines pass each other on Powell Street. So this one gang, in blue, jumped on at Eddy and started yelling at the other gang, in red, and before you could say anything – if you dared – they were shooting their hand guns from the goddamned cable car! The reason? The ones wearing red were pissed that the ones wearing blue were in "their territory." Who appointed them King Ferdinand of Spain?! Fuck "their" territory!

I didn't count the number of bullets exchanged. To be honest I just watched with my mouth open. I could not believe it. These eight guys were hiding behind some of the poles and ducking behind the seats, then popping up like they were in a "Fast and Furious." Pow! Pow! Most of them were lousy shots. The passengers on both cable cars got down on the floor and covered their heads. One woman was trying to shelter her baby from the gun fire and kept waving at the shooters. Hey didn't give a shit about her baby. They cared that somebody was wearing the "wrong" color! I wanted to have a gun so bad I could taste it. I'd blow the whole bunch of them away so fast they'd shit all over their fucking red or blue colors! But, as I said before, we're not allowed to carry weapons to work. I might get one anyway.

Bitty the Second, the pet rat that Darlene gave me, was terrified at the noise the guns were making, even though the gangs were on different cable cars. He doesn't even like it when I ring my gripman's bell. Now and then he scrambles around inside my jacket and even scratches my left tit a little. "Easy, boy!" I tried to comfort him. "Easy!"

The whole episode didn't last more than a couple of minutes, if that. The good news is that both gangs jumped off the cars and ran away. The bad news is that a guy in a passing SUV happened to have a shotgun in his truck and jumped out, vigilante style, and started taking pot shots at the bad guys. He managed to hit one of them in the leg and that Bastardo Assholla ran off limping. Yay! But the guy in the SUV also shot two passengers, one a grandmother in her eighties, who died later, and half-crippled an off-duty security guard who was so traumatized by the events around him he couldn't get his own gun out.

Later they caught five of the gang members involved, but they weren't deported. San Francisco is a fucking "Sanctuary City" and the bleeding hearts wouldn't let them be sent packing, because they were "poor" and "disenfranchised" and probably also "incest survivors" and suffering from "Asperger's Syndrome." The whole thing burned the hell out of my ass-burger, I'll tell you that. If we're not more careful, we are going to kill ourselves with Political Correctness! Mark my words! It's a sad, sad state when it's considered worse to call something awful what it is than to *be* what it is!

03 80

I can't tell if my life sucks or not. On the one hand, compared to some starving, maggot-eyed baby in sub-Saharan darkest Africa, I'm doing very well. I have an "interesting" job, I suppose. I watch TV programs on a 46-inch screen (too much TV), and have a crock pot that turns out a mean corn on the cob, and even a popcorn popper. On the other hand, I have no friends, all my relatives are dead, my "girlfriend" is nowhere to be seen. I haven't had sex in so long my dangler is shriveled and nestled up like a polar bear cub in hibernation. Maybe it's the cold snap we've been having as well. It at least used to dangle, for God's sake.

They say the un-examined life is not worth living. More likely it's the only life worth living! I don't know what to do about it, except keep my head down and keeping plowing ahead: off to work, home from work, off to work, back from work. (Was that a special booger on the brake lever today?!)

I think this woman on the cable car today was flirting with me. Maybe it would have led to something. But I'd be ashamed to have her see my dangler the way it is now, and I'd probably shoot in a minute or less because it's been so long. Besides, the woman had a wall-eye, if that's what you call it. You know, one eye pulled off to the side. I find that creepy. Sorry.

I just got a phone call on my smart phone from Darlene's apartment manager. He said they found Darlene unconscious inside her fireplace, on the hearth. She wasn't burned, thank the Lord, but she was all covered in soot. Darlene loves that fireplace. In fact, she rented the apartment primarily because of that fireplace. Apparently she's had another one of her "spells," like the one where I had to have her carted off to the Emergency Room. This time she had been laying there – lying there? – for over a day. They only found her because her rent was overdue and the manager wouldn't give up until he roused her. It's a good thing Darlene hadn't paid on time or she might be dead.

I'm trying to decide whether to go visit her in the hospital or not. She hasn't asked for me. The manager knew my name and found my number in Darlene's address book. I suppose I should rush over to see her. We could gush and hug and make up and live happily ever after, like in a chick flick. Perhaps we could even live together, finally, actually get married legally.

Except that Darlene is very, very messy. She's almost what they call a "hoarder." She won't throw anything away, even flyers from grocery stores with expired savings coupons. Her entire apartment is full of junk, like old blue light bulbs that are supposed to prevent Winter Depression, an Ikea bookcase that hasn't been put together in seven years, books by L. Ron Hubbard (never read), Yogi Truths for the West (Volumes I, II, and V), cigarette butts from when she smoked for a couple of months, a collection of refrigerator magnets from Tahiti (from a flea market in Fremont), large calendars from fifteen years ago, sets of plastic dishes, old tax forms, some Raggedy Ann dolls from her childhood. You name it, it's there! Darlene gets on my nerves without actually living with her. With her, wouldn't it be a downright nightmare? She also doesn't flush after she pees. She says it's left over from when San Francisco had a drought, but I suspect she does it to spite me.

So I'm torn, you might say. Torn is not good.

ଓ ଓ

Now I feel even worse about Darlene. Her doctor tells me that she has gone into a coma. It's probably from her diabetes. No, I have not gone to visit her. Would that wake her up or just make her fade off forever?

ଓ ଓ

I swear he was a terrorist. What better to blow to smithereens than a cable car? That would get as much world-wide publicity as the twin towers did in NYC. I'm talking about this creep who looked about twenty-two years old who got on at noon today at Jackson Street. He was *not* sporting the usual gear, the long tunic, baggy pants, knitted cap, and scraggy beard. Well, maybe he did have a beard. I've heard that eye-witnesses are notoriously unreliable, and I'm living proof of it. This terrorist (person of terror?) looked right at me and I at him, and all I got was a vague, somewhat threatening image. Scraggly beards and mean stares will do that to a person. He was also carrying a back pack by its strap, not wearing it, as if he meant to store it somewhat in order for it to explode. He looked Arabic. Sorry to "racially profile," but he looked like an Arab, from Arabia! Not all Arabs are terrorists, I realize, but an awful lot of the terrorists are Arabs. Give me a break. At least let me be on my guard against the likely culprits instead of some grandma from Dubuque.

I even nodded to my conductor, Jack Chen, to keep a lookout for Mr. Terrorist. He did, so the guy seemed nervous and reluctant to act. We really haven't had enough training to deal with terrorists, just some P.C. memo from MUNI about "being sensitive to the terrorist community," or some such bullshit. I promise you if I am going to be blown to bits by somebody's bomb on my cable car, I am not going to be "sensitive." I'm going to tear their testicles off as I fly through the air, or at least make shrapnel out of my teeth and kill the fuckers back!

You get busy at times on the cable cars. For instance, something blows onto the tracks and you have to remove it or there is a spurt of passengers crowding around you. Today both things happened at the same time. Jack Chen was busy checking on some cash fares, and I had to remove a couple of spilled batteries that got stuck in the tracks. When I got back to the grip, I could no longer see my terrorist. I mouthed these words to Jack Chen: "Where is he?" He mouthed back: "I lost him." We both looked around to see if he was still on the cable car. Maybe he had jumped off when we stopped.

But, no, there he was, crouched down, fiddling with his goddamned back pack. I told myself, "You'd better go over there and see what he's up to. That's a 'terror wrist,' if I ever saw one." I wasn't positive the Patriot Act or MUNI's rules allowed me to look in somebody's back pack. Stop and frisk?!

You horrible, racist Islamophobe, you! We could wind up being sued to kingdom come. The guy looked at me as if he couldn't wait until I turned my back and he blew all of us into bits as he went straight to Heaven. What a religious dick!

But then two gay guys got on carrying Bloomingdale's shopping bags. They were an obvious couple, both in their mid-twenties, holding hands. They were handsome enough to be models. I think they may have had alcoholic cocktails at their early lunch, shall we say. They seemed quite pleased with each other, a little fem, but not that bad. They happened to stand near the terrorist and his back pack. He looked up from his fiddling just as the two gay guys started kissing – and not just lip smooching. They got those tongues in there good. It was gross and violating public standards by a mile. I almost turned away. But it caught the attention of Mr. Terrorist, who looked like he was going to puke. In fact, his hand went up to his mouth as the gay French kiss just kept going and going, like the Energizer bunny. "Stop!" he cried out, but the two didn't stop. They were really into that kiss now. Suddenly the terrorist pulled himself up by a pole, grabbed his back pack and forced his way to the exit steps. "*Allahu akbar!*" he yelled as he jumped off the cable car and ran away from the gay kiss from Hell.

I realize that he may come back another day, but today was a good day for gay liberation. (I do think those gays maybe overdid the French part of the kiss a little bit, but who am I to complain?) As maybe you can tell, I don't mind the gays – even when they "flaunt it." They tend to be colorful and don't carry guns.

C03 80

The guy today was gay, but not a flaunter, a reasonable-looking fellow about thirty, with an all-American face, trim little body, and a back pack. He was not a terrorist. He did have an agenda, though. He seemed to be a tourist with a Bucket List, literally. He wanted to see all the sights that you can see in The City by the Bay and was ticking them off on a list he held in his left hand. I chatted him up a bit and asked what he had seen so far. He gushed about Coit Tower and its murals, the Cliff House, the old Golden Gate Bridge and the new Bay Bridge, about North Beach, Top of the Mark, and the views from Land's End toward the Marin coastline. I sort of envied him. I guess I had gotten too jaded. He had, like so many before him, forgotten or never known that a summer in San Francisco means it will be COLD. So he was wearing a short-sleeved shirt and shorts. He was freezing, but he was so happy and busy checking off his list, he didn't seem to notice.

"What have you got left to do on your list?" I asked him as we reached the end of the line, up on Jackson.

"Just two things," he replied. "Chinatown and the Castro."

"Both disappointing," I said.

"I hope not."

"A lot of hype."

"Really?" He seemed pained to hear that the rest of his Bucket List was going to be a bust.

"Maybe when it's your first time, it won't be so bad," I relented. Christ, who likes a killjoy! KILLJOY WAS HERE!!

"There is one other thing on my list," he said, almost shyly, not quite.

"Oh?"

"Now I've done the cable car."

"I hope it wasn't a disappointment."

"No, not at all."

"Well, this is the end of the line," I said. My conductor and the two remaining other passengers jumped off and hurried away on whatever errands they had. The Guy with the Bucket List stayed on. "It's the end of the line!" I said again.

He gave me a smile. "There is *one* other thing on my list that I haven't *done*," he said. He gave me a second smile.

"You're kidding?" I said.

"It's something I always wanted to do. And you're perfect."

"Am I reading this right?" I asked.

"Looks pretty dark inside there." He pointed.

I steered the car into the barn. It was a Sunday night, approaching midnight, pretty much vacated in the terminal.

I turned to face my passenger. We both double-checked to make sure we were alone. He got down into the driver's well and I unzipped my pants and turned to meet my fetishistic new best friend. He was very good, and I was very horny. It didn't take much time. The cable cars have seen far worse than a blow job, let me tell you!

I hate porn. I feel left out, and it's so exaggerated. Those guys' dicks are ridiculous. I think they're photo-shopped or something. But if I'm IN the porn, that's a different story. The guy even said, upon departing, "You're one sexy dude!" And I didn't even have to buy him dinner! Yay San Francisco! (Naturally I thought about poor Darlene the whole time. . . Like fuck. No, I didn't! I'm a man!)

You know what else? Time's a-ticking, and there are no orgasms in Hell! (It was also one of the greatest bj's of all time, and they ought to put up a plaque.)

ଓ ଅ

Speaking of real terror, this afternoon some ugly-ass woman in her late fifties was on her cell phone talking at the top of her lungs on my cable car. Other passengers were giving her looks, but this doll was clueless that she might be disturbing others. In fact, I think she enjoyed disturbing others. She wasn't calling about some emergency, either, like maybe a terrorist onboard! She was jabbering on and on about her toenails! She couldn't decide whether she should get pink or dark red nail polish. I think she was talking to her daughter, maybe in New York. She had a very heavy New York accent, you know "forgeddaboutit," which was bearable (maybe) right after 9/11, but not before and not since. She sounded like a thug, and she was.

Finally, I'd had enough and I spoke up. "Madam, please! Your voice carries." I started to point at the little sign that read BE KIND. NO CELLPHONES IN USE ONBOARD. Somebody had defaced it, and it was unreadable.

"You're not the boss of me," the old biddy snapped back. She moved her cell phone to her other ear. "Some asshole driver is hassling me," she informed her listener. "I knew I would hate San Francisco!"

"Madame," I persisted," you are annoying the staff and the other passengers."

She looked back over her shoulder and gave me the finger. At the same time two hulking men who were sitting next to the harpy with their backs toward me started to rise from their seats, slowly turning around with glares on their ugly thug faces. "You can't talk to our mother like that," one of them said.

I gulped. I mean, these guys were six-seven, six-eight, in their mid-thirties, and they were making fists at me about a yard away. I could not believe it. "I'm going to have to ask you to leave the cable car if you don't put away that cell phone," I managed, my vocal cords rather pinched.

Momma Brute waved at me snottily and said, "Oh, I have to deal with my daughter here. She just came out as a lesbian!" Her daughter wasn't coming out as a lesbian. The old broad was mocking me and the way my voice had cracked.

In my own defense, let me say that I don't usually have to ask many people to behave on the cable cars, aside from the occasional gang or terrorist, and so I was taken aback at the resistance I was getting from the Domestic Terror Trio. "This is your final warning," I added.

Brute Son Number 2 stood and turned around fully now, holding a pole, and stared me up and down, while Brute Son Number 1 reached into his coat pocket. Momma Brute said to her cell phone, "Yanko and Ratko are taking care of it. Don't worry about your mother, Krazmira."

Where was my backup? Just this old Greek woman named Athena who rode sometimes, sitting off to the side, deaf as a doorpost and brain-addled to boot. A hell of a lot of good she'd be in this fight!

I was almost reconciled to being shot, strangled, or both by Yanko and Ratko. But when Ratko saw the fear in my eyes, he merely raised his arm and did a "limp wrist" gesture at me. The son of a bitch! I was a sissy? I was a sissy because it was just me against these two Krakens from Hell's Kitchen? Even their fucking Momma probably had a stun gun in her cell phone!

I wish I could say I leapt at their throats and killed all three of them, like in some god-damned cool video game or some Anglo-Saxon "chronicle," inflicting grievous damage upon them with my gun-penis. But all I did was piss my pants. At least it was after they had left, and they didn't see the stain. So there!

What's happening to the quality of life in my world? Less cell phones! More orgasms!

ⓒ ⓑ

I have been told that Darlene is still in her coma, "resting comfortably, out of Intensive Care." I will go see her any day now. It's hard enough talking to her when she's awake, never mind in a coma. I bet if I started talking to her, she'd start flailing about and do herself some real damage – or me.

Just when I thought things might have settled down into a routine so that I could rest my frazzled mind – I do worry about Darlene. I do care about her. – somebody goes and leaves a big turd on my cable car. It was on the floor under a seat in the middle. I picked it up and put it in a plastic bag. I figured that it was a dog turd, but then when I looked at it more carefully, I was sure it was a human one. Now who would shit on a cable car?! I ask you. I don't think Momma Brute had had time to! Probably the inclination, just not the time.

I tried to jump off several times when we were stopped, to throw it into a garbage bin along the route, although you are supposed to separate "your compost" from "your paper items," as if I had time to get the shit 'just so.' But there was a cop on one corner and a shop owner on the next, neither looking forgiving for any "compost infringement"! So I held onto the bag. Bitty the Second, under my arm, could smell it and sniffed curiously. I pushed his head back and told him to go to sleep.

My mind turned to ruminations on just how that human turd got to where it was on my cable car at 10:33 on a Thursday on an early spring day.

Was somebody refused the use of a restaurant's restaurant? It happens a lot, actually. Was the turd a political statement? Let My People Shit!

Maybe the outdoor public toilet down the hill wasn't working, as usual? The homeless sleep in it, drug addicts shoot up in it, tourists are shocked by the inside of it, and nobody seems to take care of it. We MUNI employees have keys to special johns here and there throughout the city, so it wasn't one of us.

Though I wouldn't put it past Mary Lou Luten, one of the MUNI inspectors. She's full of shit!

Then I thought perhaps it was from somebody from a foreign country. Yeah, yeah, call me "xenophobic" all you like. The fact is in some places people shit in a hole right in the ground. They don't even sit on a toilet. Shitting is shitting, I suppose, but squatting over a hole? Would you make your grandmother shit over a hole? What about her old, creaky legs, to say nothing about the lack of dignity?

It could have been a little kid who left the turd. Lost control, the mother didn't see it, and suddenly there it was. Well, why wasn't she watching better? Why didn't the mother pick it up? Was it the mean little ghost boy from 1909? *Boo!!*

No, it was a teenager! Teenagers will do anything!

It was probably on a dare from his buddies. "Bryce is too chicken to shit on a cable car! Nan nee nan nee noo!" I'll show you who can shit on a cable car!" Bryce bragged, and then he did it with his buddies sheltering him from view. Then they all laughed until they almost fainted and ran off and did something else obnoxious. (Am I beginning to sound like my cranky dead Aunt Mildred?)

Was it the Lurking Terrorist when he saw the two gays French kissing? Or me getting a BJ?

The blue and red gangs popped one out of their pants in the excitement of the shoot-out and nobody saw it until just now? What *color* was the turd?!

Maybe old Athena dozed off and dropped one and didn't even notice? Is my time for dropping turds coming too?

Then I realized the truth. God Almighty had placed the turd there under the seats as a test. Of course! Aunt Mildred was always saying that "Almighty God is testing me!" Usually she was referring to something her least-favorite nephew (me) had done, like smoking weed in the tall grass behind her house in Stockton, but if "Almighty God" could take the time out of his busy schedule to test my Aunt Mildred, then He certainly could take time out to test me too.

And I survived that test. I saw a green plastic garbage bin labeled for COMPOST at the top of Nob Hill, and, glory be, if I didn't toss that turd into that bin and slammed the lid shut on it. In my mind that turd was no more! I hadn't let it get me down for more than a few minutes, and my life went on. That's how you have to deal with all the shit life brings you.

Thank you, God!

ღ ჯ

Do you remember the elderly twin sisters I told you about before, Clarice and Clementine Jones? I had lunch with Clarice that one time, and she turned out to be even less Politically Correct than me. She was the one who donated her one kidney to her sister. Well, she died, naturally, a few months ago at eighty-five.

Today I saw the other one, Clementine, on my cable car. She didn't look good, even with a new kidney. She looked every bit of her eighty-five years, despite the garish rouge and lipstick. Her face seemed skeletal and a bit jaundiced. She was wearing the sisters' famous red outfit. Luckily, no Blue Bastardos gang members saw her or they would have finished her off in a hail of bullets. The poor woman looked incredibly lonely, and I tried to chat her up a bit. "Good to see you out and about!" I called back to her.

She didn't respond.

I tried again. "I was sorry to hear about your sister."

Clementine's watery old eyes found mine, and then she even got up, raising herself laboriously with both hands. Very unsteadily she walked up to me and sat down nearby. I glanced over. "Keep your eyes on the track!" she said, fake bossy.

"Yes, M'am," I said.

"Are you the one who took Clarice out to lunch before she died?"

"I am indeed." I resisted being a smart aleck and saying, "No, I'm the one who took Clarice out to lunch after she died!"

"She said she enjoyed that lunch, even though she found you to be one of those San Francisco bleeding hearts liberals."

"Me? No, I'm a Stockton boy, heart and soul."

"Maybe it's the different generations," Clementine replied.

"It was very kind of your sister to donate to you," I gushed on.

"What are you talking about?" The old face went puckery with disdain.

"The kidney donation," I said.

"Oh, did she tell you that story?" Clementine laughed dismissively.

"She didn't give you a kidney?"

"She only had one kidney herself. So how could she give me one?"

I hemmed and hawed. "I thought that's why she died, because she gave up her one kidney for you."

"Oh, God, she loved to make people think she was so damn generous." Clementine shook her head.

"So there was no kidney donation at all? Is that what you're saying?"

"Clarice had a vivid imagination. You never knew what she might say, just to get a rise out of people."

"And you're her twin, right?" I all but winked at her.

"No, I am the sane one. Clarice was very, very unreliable." She sighed. "I still miss her, though. Our apartment seems so empty without her. I think about getting a parrot just so I can have something to worry about."

I started to say, identical twins most likely have about the same life span so maybe she should hold off on the parrot. But even I can ease up on the honesty sometimes.

"Yes, a parrot can make everything seem a little brighter," I chirped on, like Little Mary Sunshine.

"Oh, no, I'd want a mean parrot, a selfish one that would refuse to get onto my finger, one that would bite me if I rubbed its head."

"Really?" I thought about showing her Bitty the Second warm and cozy in my armpit, but I wasn't sure that I could trust Clementine not to turn me in.

"Since Clarice passed away, I have learned that I actually enjoyed how much trouble she was. I used to scream at her and sometimes even hated her. Now everything is calm, peaceful, and as boring as can be."

"You need a husband!" I joked.

"Are you volunteering?" Clementine joked back.

"Well, my girlfriend is in a coma," I said. "Maybe it's time to start lookin'."

"I never had sex in my life," Clementine went on.

Too Much Information! . . . Too Little Information? "It's never too late." I sounded like an absolute idiot.

Clementine cocked her head and said, "Are you trying to 'hit on' me, is that the word?"

Lord, deliver me from my own mouth! How do you explain to a grieving eight-five-year-old walking virgin corpse that you didn't mean to 'hit on" her?! I certainly was not hitting on her, and yet I didn't want her to think that the idea of hitting on her was too grotesque for me to contemplate for even a second. Good grief, the woman had enough problems already without me piling another one on.

Thankfully, Clementine shook her old head and smiled. "That's very thoughtful of you, but I am afraid I must decline your offer."

I gulped. Which way to go with this now? "Hey, Granny, that was no offer of a sex date, and don't you dare put me on your booty call list!" "I am sorry, Ms. Jones, but there has been a terrible misunderstanding about what you think I just said to you. I just spoke up because you looked so miserable, old, and lonely."

What I wound up saying was: "My loss! You can't win 'em all, I guess."

Clementine liked that. She had a big, broad smile on her face. "I have to get off at the next stop," she said. "I want to watch 'Days of Our Lives' if it's still on!"

"Maybe we'll have that hot date next time."

I flashed the biggest, phoniest smile you have ever seen on this planet. Thank you, Governor from the Republic of Texas!

"Oh, you won't see me again, kind sir, most likely. I think it's time for me to join my sister on the other side."

"Oh, don't say that!"

"I don't mind. It's actually my time to go." As she stepped off the cable car, she pulled her collar up against a sudden blast of wind. "Just remember, young man, every misery isn't bad for you," she said as she stepped into the street.

I never did see her again. I can guess what happened to her.

The more I think about it, the more I think she's right. Every misery isn't bad for you.

CB BO

I try not to be overly friendly with our customers, as you can probably tell. You have to strike a balance between being a cold-prick Public Employee and some goofball glad-hander. I think I manage most days. But today a gentleman stretched my limits.

I don't know his name, but he rides occasionally, down Powell Street and not up. Today he was riding up.

I'd say he's about sixty, Caucasian, with frosted brown hair. There are traces of old, teenage acne scars on both cheeks, not terrible but noticeable. He ordinarily wears a business suit, so I assume he is in some business or other. He's never offered me a discount, so I can't say for sure! Generally, he is quiet and unobtrusive. Today he was carrying an urn in a box on his lap. At least that's what he said it was. "My brother's ashes," he informed me, pointing to the box.

"Hmm," I said.

"Really!" The man flashed the urn, which looked to be genuine marble, gray and white.

"Interesting," I said in a non-committal way.

"He died of liver cancer. He was only fifty-nine."

"I'm sorry to hear that."

"He was an alcoholic. Ruined his liver. Used to be very handsome."

I couldn't resist. "Are you taking his ashes somewhere in particular?"

"I'm meeting my two sisters, to have a ceremony at a park on Nob Hill. My brother, Jerry, always loved to smoke dope there. He didn't leave a will, but he did ask for a scattering of his ashes. I'm afraid I'm running a little late. My dentures broke." He pointed self-consciously to his mouth. He was barely opening it because his partial in the front was missing.

"I'm sure it will be very nice," I said. I don't really get why people want to have their ashes spilled in a park or even into the sea. God knows where you end up! In some fish's gut! A grave is good enough for me. But to each his own, I guess.

"My younger sister, Arlene, has flown down from Vancouver Island to be part of it. I haven't seen her in four years. My big sister, Madge, has arranged it all. She loves to arrange things." There was a bit too much emphasis on the word *loves*. I had been warned.

He rode the rest of the way in silence. He was weeping, however. The tears stuck in the edges of his eyes.

"Well, have a nice scattering," I managed as he got off my cable car.

To my surprise, he was back on the car before we even began the descent down Powell again.

"They did it without me," the man complained. He was still holding the box with the urn.

"What?"

"They didn't wait."

"But didn't you have the ashes?"

"They had some already. I found the place where they scattered theirs. But Madge and Arlene were nowhere to be found."

"What happened?"

"I was late. I swear it was only about twenty minutes. I broke my partial just before I was to leave home. I was eating some almonds. But they couldn't wait!" The man's tears had dried up, and his face was suffused with rage.

"Can't you meet up with them later perhaps?"

"I've had it with Madge! I hate her guts!"

I know better than to get involved in family disputes, especially when it's not even my family. "I'm sure it will sort itself out," I said.

"I'm sending her a text message right now." Sure enough, the gentleman had taken out his cell phone and was typing away. On and on went the message. I was tempted to say, "You'd better not put so much in one message."

But before I could, the man was cursing. "I lost it! I lost it!"

"Maybe if it was written in anger, it's best if . . ."

"No, it went through. Arlene has responded already." He held up the cell phone so that I could see it. "Listen to what that bitch said!" the man almost screamed.

"I'd really rather not," I mumbled.

He read his sister's message to me anyway: "'We were on a schedule. It's not all about you, Jake! You have quite the nerve hurling accusations at us. You should be ashamed of yourself. You were the one who was late to your own brother's scattering! Not us!'"

Jake looked at me with total outrage on his face.

"I called her and told her I would be late because of my broken teeth! She can't wait twenty minutes for her own brother?!"

I shrugged, sort of in agreement, I suppose.

Jake went back to his cell phone and began texting furiously again. Obviously long-simmering family dynamics were in play here.

I turned my full attention through the well to the tracks below me. We were in one of the steeper grades on Powell Street now.

But Jake had found a sympathetic ear, or at least an ear, and he was not letting go of it. "Listen to what I texted her," he demanded. I shook my head, but he didn't care. "You think you're such a fucking saint, but you aren't, Madge! You did a lousy job on Mom's estate. You actually stole Mom's gold coins, and those were part of the estate, not just the house! Jerry and I both thought you were a fucking thief! How do you manage to sleep at night?! We know that you don't approve of our drinking, but who the Hell appointed you our mother!?"

Almost before Jake's message could have gotten through, Madge was back with her rage. "Look what's she says!" Jake shouted to me, reading his sister's words aloud. "'How dare you criticize me! I sleep just fine at night. Who never called Mom when she was dying? Who barely saw his own brother when he was in the hospice? Who took care of Aunt Loopy when she had to go into the home? Me! That's who! Me! I did all the dirty work of this goddamn family of drunks. Thank Heaven, at least Arlene and I are not god-damned drunks! And it was you who tried to steal your brother's stamp collection, taking the one thing he had to give to his two boys! Who's the fucking thief? YOU! That's who!'"

Jake hopped on that cell phone before you could say "Instant Communication." "Those were my stamps, most of them! Jerry stole them from ME when we lived at the Fox Plaza for that year. All I asked for was a few fucking STAMPS that were already mine! And don't you dare drag Arlene into this. I am not angry with her, and don't you make her think I am. It's you, Miss Goody Two-Shoes. You don't care for the way Jerry and I drink. Fuck you! Maybe I don't care about many cookies and cakes you eat! You are two tons of non-fun, and I worry every day that you might collapse from any number of horrible diseases, heart disease being the least of them. Madge, you are

GROSSLY overweight, and no one will have the heart to point it out to you, not even Arlene. Plus, you have those seventeen hideous moles all over your back plus that psoriasis on your neck and hands. No wonder no man has ever wanted you for a minute!'" Jake held up his cell phone for me to approve.

Poor Aunt Loopy. Did the family drive her Loopy or was she already there? I wondered.

There was a ping from Jake's cell phone. "She's written back! 'Jake, you are losing your mind, no doubt from all the alcohol you consume. I've seen you deteriorating for years. You look worn out and old. How dare you throw these false accusations against me and Arlene! I handled Mom's estate like a professional. She told me on her deathbed that she wanted her gold coins to go "to the girls." She had seen what you two boys would do with the money — drink it up like there's no tomorrow! And I am not FAT! I HAVE WORKED LIKE HELL TO LOSE THIRTY POUNDS AND THIS IS THE REWARD I GET! Why are you being so mean? What happened to all your so-called religious principles — all that meditation shit you claim you do. Don't write me back unless you have kind things to say! You have broken your sister Arlene's heart!'"

Jake was holding his cell phone out in front of him. The brother's ashes fell to the floor of the cable car. They didn't spill, but they might just as well have. "Listen to this! Listen to this!" he ordered me. "You are a thief and a hypocrite! You justify your illegal actions because you are so Holier Than Thou! Well, let me tell you something – YOU'RE NOT HOLY! AND YOU ARE DEAD TO ME! GOT THAT, BITCH? DEAD TO ME!!!! You CUNT!!'"

Jake looked at me for approval before he was to push Send. "What do you think?" he asked me.

"I don't think CUNT is going to go over very well," I muttered.

Jake didn't really need my approval. He slammed a thumb on Send, and off flew his terminal message. "Now I have lost my brother and my big sister both. And Arlene will probably side with Madge, so I've lost her too. What a wonderful day!" He stood up, looked at his cell phone, and then threw it as hard as he could from the cable car. I think it didn't kill anyone, except maybe the family involved.

ন্ধ ৪০

Some might say that I am xenophobic, but I am not, not really. Yeah, we are a Nation of Immigrants, but when more than half your population changes into other people with different body types, different customs, many of them nasty, and their own prejudices, superstitions, and system of bribes, you are not being "xenophobic" to be upset by it. What if you went to Italy and everybody was Albanian?! What if you went to France and everybody was Algerian?! How about a Spanish-speaking United States?

Let me tell you, not everybody who has come to San Francisco in recent years is a winner. Some of them in fact are total pricks, con men, and could not care less about God Bless America. It's all about *them*. They have learned enough English, barely, to say the things they are expected to say about freedom and justice for all, and the pursuit of happiness. Shit, they are as hard-hearted and sharp-elbowed as any you'll find in the history of the world. Yeah, yeah, I know history of full of people running over other people and taking over. But at least let me gripe when HISTORY is running across my own face!

It's hard enough keeping the cable cars free of bombs and turds. Now I have to put up with fucking parades all the time! There is the LGBT Pride Parade, of course. I guess I've grown accustomed to that one, it's been around so long. Yeah, yeah, the Lesbian, Gay,

Bi-curious, Temporary Gay, and Sucked a Dick Once Parade! It's almost as predictable and boring as the Rose Bowl Parade. There are also at least three Hispanic parades, Cinco de Mayo and Carnivale, Our Lady of the Fertile Vagina, Cinco de Mayo 2, and so on. Plus various labor groups and protests against Corporate Interests, or cops, or even against MUNI – I can get behind that one, let me tell you. But enough is enough.

Now the goddamned anti-abortion nuts are out filling up Market Street with their Pro-Life signs and their pictures of sonograms all blown up to scare people into having even more babies! Even more parades! Yikes! Every time I see Dr. Drew or some other pious TV "M.D." talking about saving African babies I think: MY GOD, PLEASE! WE CAN'T HANDLE THE AFRICAN BABIES WE HAVE NOW! ENOUGH BABIES OF ALL TYPES!

And when the pro-lifers start blocking my cable car so that I can't get across town, because the cars are all screwed up since Market Street is blocked, believe me it doesn't make me want not to have an abortion. It makes me want to MAKE the pro-lifers have an abortion, lots and lots of abortions, most of them retroactive!

There they are looking so holier than thou with their hand-printed signs and a bunch of busy-body priests and nuns guiding them through the un-holy streets of San Francisco. I was shocked at how many of them there are. Why the hell are they marching in San Francisco against abortion? Everybody's gay here, right??!!! We don't need contraception or abortion, because we are not reproducing!! (Okay, you're right. I had a baby with the Indian gal. If he's still alive.)

I yelled at some of them today, and they prayed for me! How dare they! They seem to think prayer is some kind of laser beam they can direct anywhere they choose, to take out enemies like me or to get special favors from the Big Pro-Lifer in the Sky. "Kill our enemies, O Lord, if it is Thy Divine Will!" "Let Mrs. McCarthy-Rodriguez recover from those suspicious lumps in her oversized breasts and have seven more babies!" "Dear Lord, help the Giants win the Super Bowl and we will have a zillion novenas for you, we pray in Jesus' name." Stop it! Just stop it! In Jesus' name, stop! We are drowning in people, and they are all blocking my cable car!

By the way, I read an article somewhere that said people who know others are praying for them die faster than others do. Moreover, there is absolutely no correlation between your little mouth uttering prayers and anything else happening in the entire universe.

What colossal chutzpah! Even if God does exist, He's too busy punishing masturbators by putting warts on their hands to listen to you.

These marchers are as bad as those Friday night bikers, out to intimate and annoy the rest of us one night a month. They'd be out every night of the week if they could. I think they're called Mass-Holes, or something like that. They are all twenty-two years and resent the hell out of any other form of transportation except the bicycle, especially their own personal bicycle. Hey, kids, some of us are too old to ride bikes anymore! Not that I ever did. Some of them don't even like cable cars. I have been deliberately bumped at least twenty times. (All right, two times.) They seem to think cable cars pollute. They run on electricity, Mass-Holes! The fucking bikers exude more toxic gases in the methane from their farting asses than the cable cars have in over a hundred years! God, people can be so self-righteous! Not me, of course. I'm right. They're wrong. End of story.

ଓଃ ଃ୧

Would you believe that "gentleman" who cussed out his sister over the scattering of their brother's ashes on Nob Hill was back on my cable car today,

189

with a brand new smart-phone? He flashed it at me. "I made up with my sister Madge," he says to me. "I told her I was sorry I called her a cunt."

"Yeah? What did she say?"

"She hasn't replied yet. She will."

"You think so?" I said.

"Or she really is a cunt," he said.

I kept out of it, as best I could. Why is it some folks won't let you keep out of their business?

ଔ ଈ

You've heard of the Birdman of Alcatraz? Well, that was some time ago. Alcatraz is closed now, for prisoners, yet way open for tourists. I get more than my share of people on the wrong cable car looking for the ferry to Alcatraz. I tell them they have to get down to the Embarcadero and find the pier that's marked: Pier 33, NOT Pier 39. That's for junk. I went to Alcatraz once and was amazed at how many people wanted to be locked into one of those little jail cells, as some sort of thrill. Tiny and cold.

It made me want to murder people. If you want a great big view of San Francisco, plus some cold and a thrill, climb aboard one of my cable cars and feast your eyes and unbutton your jacket. They should put a gambling casino out there on the Rock. I would go. Even better, give me the rights to a casino. I deserve it – I put up with tourists and I have a girlfriend in a coma!

I don't have any Birdman tales, but I did see the Michelangelo of San Quentin not that long ago. He was eighty years old and had been released from San Quentin after a whopping fifty-six years. I don't know what he did, but it must have been pretty terrible to spend that much time in prison. Or maybe they just forgot he was there. He said that he was getting out early because of "compassionate leave" or something like that. I guess the authorities figured he was too feeble now to slit anyone's throat. He was all crippled up, with a bent back, hobbling steps, eyebrows out to here, and earlobes that seemed to hang halfway to his belt.

He said that he had been released that day and was carrying all his possessions in a suitcase. He offered to show me what he had. I wasn't interested, but how are you going to refuse that?

Inside were some torn underwear, a toothbrush, a couple of worn shirts from 1944, a pair of eyeglasses, and a little purple velvet sack. That's all I could make out. "I have been carving for over fifty years,"

Michelangelo told me. He held up the velvet sack. "And this is all I have saved, my very best."

"What did you carve?" I asked.

"Oh, I carved horses and crows and seagulls and pelicans."

"Out of what?"

"Out of soap mostly. They wouldn't let us have wood or stuff like that. Too dangerous."

"To make shivs, right? Is shivs the word?"

"Yeah. I made some in my early days there. But then I shifted to art."

"Really?"

"I saw this program about sculpture on PBS, and I thought maybe I could do that."

"How great."

"I wasn't very good at first, but then something clicked and I began to carve some very good things."

"In soap, this was?"

"Not the best medium, but it was all I could get. Some guys liked my stuff, but some took it and washed their asses with it. Some just broke them for the fun of it."

"How many did you do?"

"Oh, I lost count. I had so many I lost count. The guards let me keep them under my bed. But then I was transferred to a new cell and I had to leave them behind."

"You couldn't ship them out to somebody?"

Michelangelo looked at me like I was crazy. "No, no shipping allowed."

"Then the Governor came by for a visit one day and saw your stuff and started a museum inside San Quentin! Right?"

"I don't know what you're talking about." Michelangelo scrunched up his big eyebrows.

"I was just joshin' you."

"No, I had to leave the things I had done the last few years behind. I couldn't carry them all and didn't have room in my suitcase." He patted it to show me how small it was. "I was able to save this one item." He held up the mysterious purple velvet sack that had been in his suitcase.

"And you want to sell it to me?" I said snidely. Believe me, there is no lack of con artists on the cable cars.

"You want to buy it?"

"Not really."

"Do you want to see it?"

"How much are you asking for it?"

"I hadn't thought about selling it."

"What is it a carving of?"

"It's hard to say, very modern. It's in maple wood. Some guard gave me the raw piece of wood."

"That was nice of him."

"I was going to give the carving to him, but he was strangled last month."

"In prison?"

"No, by some guys in his neighborhood. He was out of uniform at the time."

I looked Michelangelo up and down. Who was joshin' who? "And now you're thinking about selling your one last treasure, hmm?"

"It's the only thing I was able to save, out of all the things I carved over the years."

It had better be damned good! I thought. We'll arrange to put it in the Sistine Chapel! "Okay, let's see it," I said. "I have to concentrate here or we might crash." I motioned to my levers.

Michelangelo untied the string on the velvet sack and slipped the carving that was inside into his hand.

Three miraculous things then occurred.

The carving began to glow as with a Heavenly Light. For the image that had been carved was the Face of Jesus of Nazareth. Soon a Heavenly Choir of mixed-race Gospel singers jumped up on the cable car and began to sing. They had come from a service at Glide Memorial Church on Taylor. The carving left the hand of the elderly prison artist and ascended into Almighty Heaven and the Lord's powerful voice rang out: "I am well pleased with my servant's work and now I welcome him into my bosom forever." The old man then closed his eyes and passed away.

The second miracle was that the carving, of a seagull, was the most exquisite carving I have seen in my life. Its maple sheen made it seem as if the bird were just freeing itself from the piece of wood. Its eye caught the viewer's and seemed to say, "I am Joy and I will justify this old man's difficult life because this object will remain in one art museum or another forever. It will soon rival the Mona Lisa as the most viewed and venerated artwork of all time."

The third miracle was that there was indeed a carving inside the velvet sack, of a pelican's beak, maybe four inches long. Or I think it was a pelican's beak. It was the most inept carving I have ever seen in my life, something a four-year-old child would be embarrassed to show his doting parents. It looked like Michelangelo had merely hacked at the wood until some vague bird shape emerged. I don't know if he didn't have any proper tools or his hands had become so crippled from age that he couldn't manipulate whatever he was carving with. It was just . . . sad.

"Do you like it? It's the best one I ever did. So I am happy that I was at least able to save this one." The old man seemed to be speaking with complete sincerity. "I had to chew it with my teeth." He pointed at his mouth, and I could see now that he had virtually no teeth left at all.

"Oh, my God!" I exclaimed.

"You like it then?!" The man was absolutely beaming from my praise.

I gave the guy two twenties for it. In case you're wondering, that was the real miracle part – he got to this old grump's heart.

☙ ❧

I have been feeling guilty about not visiting Darlene, the woman I used to call "my girlfriend." It's been some weeks now. I have called her doctor, who keeps telling me that Darlene is going to come around. Apparently, some of the coma was "medically induced" rather than an Act of God. I suppose that's a good thing. I've heard of doctors having to break a leg bone in order to set it properly. Could be how the coma works.

Could be the same thing with a broken love affair. You have to crack it in two and then maybe it will repair itself. So I thought it was time to break it off with Darlene.

I went to see her at St. Francis Hospital, her usual hospital, or the one on her medical plan at any rate. There she was in Room 314, a private room, thank God. I didn't want to have to say what I was going to say to a roomful of other people. Darlene looked rested. I guess she should have; she'd been asleep for ages. The lines in her fifty-eight-year-old face had softened. That pinched area just above and between the eyes looked less severe. An orderly or someone had braided her hair, and she looked sort of like a Heidi doll from the past, only a bit fuller-faced. I couldn't see much of the "gypsy blood." There were tubes and all that shit in the way.

"Darlene?" I said.

She did not stir.

I looked at the medical paraphernalia around her single bed: a hanging drip of some kind of nutrition, I think, and a needle taped to her wrist. She probably had a catheter too, but I didn't check. I mean, really, you can have TMI!

"Darlene, it's me."

This time she moved her arm. It might have been a shrug, but I took it to be a sign of life.

"I've been thinking about us," I went on.

No reaction.

"I'm wondering if you're feeling the same way I am."

No reaction.

"I think we've been growing apart, and for some time now." I looked to see if her eyelids might flutter. "Don't you?"

A nurse with a gurney went past the open door and looked in at me. I gave her a feeble smile of acknowledgement. She moved on.

"Darlene, can you even hear me?" I wasn't at all sure. "I'm trying to find out how you feel about the two of us." She made a sound that was like a cough, only briefer, softer. "Sometimes I think we should let each other go."

I don't know what I expected – either for her to open her eyes and say, "I love you more than life itself!" or to open her eyes and say, "Yes, we haven't liked each other in years and years. Thank you for what we once had. And goodbye."

Instead, she just laid there. It crossed my mind that somebody had to clean up Darlene when she had to poop. I was glad that I didn't work in a hospital. Unless you call the cable cars a mental ward!

What if Darlene became a vegetable permanently and her insurance ran out? What if the hospital released her and I had to look after her as she laid there in that state, cleaning up her poop? What if she wasn't really a vegetable, but fully awake and paralyzed, like in some Edgar Rice Poe story about being entombed alive! She would be screaming inside her immobilized body: "Kill me! Kill me!" And then I would suffocate her, and I'd go on trial, and . . .

What if she recovered, and then later I went into a coma? Darlene would take care of me. I know she would.

. . . Wouldn't she? She'd clean up my poop. She wasn't nearly as squeamish about such things as I was.

I had never stood so still in my entire life before, and yet my mind was racing like a wildfire. Was I being a heel? A total shit? Of course I was, trying to break off with my girlfriend when she was in a coma. But for God's sake, was it right to stay chained to a living corpse forever just because it was the Noble Thing to Do?! Perhaps hearing my voice disturbed Darlene, tormented her, just as she had tuned out in some kind of comforting peace?

I couldn't stand the dilemma I was in for another day. Better to be a total shit than in limbo. So I opened my mouth, bent down toward Darlene's left ear and started to say my last goodbye to her.

Just then a senior, self-important doctor and some interns or medical students came into the room. They looked me up and down like I was a necrophiliac. To be honest, I was beginning to feel like a necrophiliac. It wasn't sex, but I was certainly trying to fuck my "girlfriend."

"We wanted to examine this patient," the self-important doctor informed me. He might as well have said, "Get the hell out of here, creep!" The rest of them waited for me to leave.

I started to bend down to kiss Darlene on the forehead, but I stopped myself. I reached inside my jacket and lifted the sleeping Bitty the Second out, held him up so that the medical team could see him, and then let him kiss Darlene. At least he brushed his whiskers against her cheek. "She loves my rat!" I barked at them. Bet they had never seen that before!

Then I took out the ugly carving that I had bought from Michelangelo of San Quentin and placed it on her pillow. I had almost forgotten it was in my pocket. "She's my beloved fiancée," I said, hoping to make them feel self-conscious.

A kiss from a rat and a crummy, inept, tooth-gnawed pelican sculpture – okay, not much to give, I realize. But at least I did not leave Darlene!

ଔ ଞ

Sometimes I wish Darlene would wake up and ride on my cable car again. I enjoyed that even more than I knew at the time, now that we can't do it anymore. We'd share little jokes about the passengers, kinda like I'm doing with you. Do you want to be my girlfriend? Hah!

On the other hand, Darlene is not in danger from the crackpots that increasingly invade my cable car. There are just too many drunks. And these are the normal, everyday people, not gang members. For instance, on three separate occasions today, "sports fans" jumped aboard, waving banners and flags, popping corks on champagne bottles, slugging beer out of cans. It seems the 49ers almost won the Super Bowl. Woopee!

Now I care as much as the next guy when my hometown team runs back and forth with an oblong-shaped ball. I have been known to shout myself hoarse at a game. But I do it at the game. I don't carry it over to the goddamned cable cars! It makes you wonder what their lives are like, if they get so much vicarious pleasure out of other men running back and forth with BALLS! In the grand scheme of things, ball-games are trivial. Why don't people get that excited about a cure for baldness or a book of cable car tales? Huh?

On the early evening run, just as it was getting dark, some of these "fans" once again set fire to the front of the cable car ahead of mine. They had torn down a bus's electricity pole and then ripped it off and used it to block the entire cable car. They piled some trash onto everything and doused it with gasoline. Guess what?! It went up in flames immediately. There were still some passengers who couldn't get off. It even burned mopey Larry Leamington, the conductor, when his pant leg caught on fire. He finally managed to snuff it out and jumped into the street. No, he didn't wait until all the passengers got off first. We are not like captains of ships, thank God!

People seemed to think the fire, the damage was hilarious. You could see their drunken, happy faces lit up by the booze and the fire. They were destroying a bus and a cable car to demonstrate how PROUD they were. Don't they have any idea how much those things cost? Hundreds of thousands of dollars, that's how much!

No, it wasn't the whole crowd doing the damage. In fact, it was just four or five. If I'd had a gun, I would have shot them. Maybe those NRA types are correct: Doesn't the Second Amendment say "A well-regulated cable car, being necessary to a free state, the right of a MUNI employee to shoot mother-fuckers shall not be infringed, without regard to race, creed, or color"?

I'm sorry I'm becoming such a nag. But I care about my city. I care! And my city is getting away from me, and I am not allowed to complain, at least not aloud.

cs ∞

This morning I had an early shift. No sooner had Tim Plucca and I taken the cable car out of the barn at Mason and Hyde and started our run, some old fat white guy jumped on and plunked himself down in a seat beside me and sat on his hands. I glanced back to make eye contact with Plucca. He rolled his eyes. I rolled mine. The old fat white guy looked a bit loony, dressed in a San Francisco Giants baseball uniform, orange and black, with a player's name stitched across his back: POSEY. I was pretty sure it wasn't Buster Posey, the catcher, who was sitting there on his hands. It was some "fan" imposter with a huge butt. He had his baseball cap turned all the way around to the back, making him look like an old-man teenage dork. Are people still using the word "dork?" Well, they should be! It was only February!

"I'm glad I caught the first car of the day," Old Timer says to me, turning to the side.

"Yeah? Why's that?" I answered.

"I've got to ensure that the Giants win the pennant again."

"Really?"

"You don't believe me?"

"Sure, I believe every word you say." I was pissing the old guy off, I could tell, but did I care?

"That's how we won the last two," he said.

"Oh, you play for the team? Or maybe you're the manager?"

"Naw. I'm too old."

"You don't look a day over seventy," I said.

"I'm sixty-nine," he said.

"Okay, I'll bite. How did you ensure that the Giants won the pennant?"

"I've figured out that if I catch the first cable car on the second Monday on the fourth month after the last win in the World Series and sit on my hands between the start and the end of the run, then we'll win!"

I turned my head to examine him. No, he wasn't foaming at the mouth. "It's a good thing you don't have to work then," I said.

"That's what I think."

"How much do the Giants pay you for doing this?"

"Oh, they don't pay me anything. I do it because I love the team."

"Who are the team this time around?" I jabbed. I watched the Giants a lot, and they were barely the same players from one year to the next, and almost none of them were American. Team? What team? Mercenaries, not team.

The Old Timer didn't seem to catch my drift. "Don't you follow the Giants?" he said. "They're great!" God, that old man was so damn happy!

"Well, you keep up the good work," I finally said.

"I usually touch those steering sticks too," he said.

He was pointing. "You mean the grip here?" I asked.

"The last gripper let me touch it."

I couldn't resist saying, "Okay, here's one for the gripper."

He was already standing next to, slightly behind, me. "Can I really?"

"I suppose."

"Wait!" The Old Timer reached down and pulled up his sock tops, one black and one orange. "This is the most important part of it," he told me.

"Oh, for Christ's sake" I swore. "You are *not* going to help the Giants win the pennant with your socks!" I shouted.

The Old Timer almost fell over backwards. His eyelids flapped and he turned pale. "You're wrong. It's worked twice before."

"You cannot control the pennant with your magic socks, or any of the rest of it!"

"It's people like you who are destroying San Francisco! And America!" he spat.

"Get a grip on reality, Grandpa!" I yelled.

The Old Timer steeled himself and then slapped his gnarly old mitt of a hand against the grip I was steering with and went back to his seat and sat with his hands under his ugly old fat white butt until the end of the line.

We didn't say anything else to each other, and he didn't thank me when he got off the car, like many did.

No, the Giants did not win the pennant again later that year. Surprise!

Unfortunately the Old Timer jumped from a cable car and under a bus when the Giants didn't win and in fact came in near the bottom. Good grief, it's a *ballgame*! And I thought my life was desperate.

Actually I think the little ghost boy from 1909, wearing a ball boy's *Gigantes* uniform, pushed the Old Timer off the car. You can still hear the mixed eerie laughter of the little boy and cries of the Old Timer at the Old Ballpark (whatever name it has now) just as the gulls arrive at the end of each and every game.

You want your superstitions. There you go.

Go Giants!

Go Ghost Boy!

CB BO

I'm guess I am becoming nothing but a grump in my older years. "Becoming??" I can hear some voices shouting. Well, in my defense, let me just say, did you ever look at the comments on YouTube or places like that? People are positively vicious. Somebody uploads a video of a kitten, and somebody called AxeMurderer23 posts: "If I could get youre kitty, Id put it in my MEAT GRINER." [sic] Sick is right! If you say, "I like yoghurt," somebody else, sometimes dozens of them, will post: "You're a COCKSUXCKING FAG COMMIE!!!! Come down here and see whatll happen to you're fucking yogurt!!!"

Civility? Where did that go? If you ask me, there was never a whole lot of civility in the first place. People just kept their evil opinions in their evil hearts. Now they can spew them all over the Internet and hide behind some moniker like BigDaddyFU-UP. How courageous! At least when I say something, I say it under my own name. (Have you noticed I have never mentioned my name in this book? He, he!)

On the cable cars I have noticed the same thing happening. People used to put their litter in the litter basket. Or they would crumple it up and take it with them. Nowadays they toss it hither and thither like animals, off the cars, onto the car floors. I feel sorry for the cleaning crews at night at the barn, who have to clean up all kinds of crap. Pardon me, for being so narrow-minded and un-accepting of other people's wonderful, international customs!

But I especially dislike seeing people spit on the cable cars. And spit they do! Even women. Never mind the TB that can be spread, it's just downright disgusting to see women or men spewing their germ-laden saliva on the floor where other people have to step in it. Sometimes they even spit on the seats! Hello! Didn't they ever hear of a handkerchief?! Or swallow the fucking stuff. Don't share it with the rest of us. You nasty, lazy, infected, selfish sons of bitches! (What name did I leave out?) The next time I catch you doing it, I swear I'm going to push you off the cable car to your deaths!

With love,

Yours sincerely, SPITTERKILLER39.

P.S. When I come on a cable car (that one time) I make sure not to spill a drop!

ᗥ ᗤ

Which brings me to tattoos. I don't get them. Why are so many people who aren't cannibals "decorating" their flesh with ink markings? Believe me, Leo DaVinci is not working in any tattoo parlor that I can determine. Scorpions, serpents, Devil skulls, passages from the Bible, the complete Koran, the complete works of porn star Ron Jeremy, you name it, it's on somebody's arm, even their neck or face. Yikes! One drunk guy even showed me a tattoo on his dick! I kid you not. It was a rosebud. He swore it grew into a sequoia tree under the right conditions. Yeah, sure. At the Resurrection on the Last Day.

One day these folks are going to regret having that tattoo of Che Gueverra right under their ear, and I don't mean at Armageddon. I mean, when they go for a job interview and I'm the boss. "What the fuck is that?" I'll ask. "Have that removed if you want to work here."

"It's my free speech," they'll claim.

"Horseshit. It's my free speech to tell you to get rid of that desecration on your skin."

"I can cover it up."

"No, you can't! Customers will still see it. What are you going to cover it with? One of those hijabs that Muslim women wear?"

"No. Those are religious."

"I don't care what they are. I'm not having any whatsoever where I'm the boss."

"Perhaps you shouldn't be the boss then," one of those smart-alecks will say.

"Oh, yeah?"

"Yeah."

"We seem to be at a standstill, aren't we?"

"So do I get the job?"

"Does the Pope have a tattoo on his butt when he shits in the woods?"

"What!?"

"We've got to nip this fad in the bud before people wind up with their entire bodies covered in doodles!" I will argue rationally.

"I think you're of an older generation. Times are changing." The tattooed one will look at me with contemptuous pity.

"Not every fad lasts, you know, pal."

"This one will."

"The biggest job in the future is going to be tattoo removal. You mark my words!"

"So do I get the job or not?"

"Tattoos are against the rules."

"No, they're not. I looked up the rules."

I'll be stumped for a moment. "Well, they should be against the rules. MUNI has a dress code, and tattoos are a form of dress."

They will look at me with beady-eyed self-assurance. "Tattoos are mainstream these days."

"I'm not hiring you with a tattoo I can see, and that's all there is to it."

There will be a small pause. "You don't follow all of MUNI's rules yourself."

"What do you mean by that?"

"What do you got under your jacket?"

"Me!"

"You also have a pet rat. Not only are animals against the rules, you are endangering your rat because you could crush it under your armpit when you put down the brake."

"He moves when he needs to," I'll say. Oops. Shit.

"I'd hate to have to report *you* to your boss," the fucker would say.

"Hey, welcome aboard!" I'll say, all shit-eating grin on my kisser.

I'll probably even get a tattoo myself, a small one out of sight, maybe on my forearm, just to be trendy – of a cable car mowing down a guy with an ugly-ass tattoo on his face! Maybe I'll get Bitty the Second a tattoo, so he won't get lost.

Maybe one for Darlene too. So that she won't get lost. Do you wander around in your mind when you're in a coma?

C33 80

I'm horny again. And my girlfriend is still in that coma. It's supposed to be a "committed relationship" even though we aren't legally married, so what am I to do? By the way, the "committed" part was Darlene's idea, not mine.

The whole thing is not a pretty picture, but I'm thinking of going to visit Darlene in her room at St. Francis and having carnal relations with her. If she was awake, she'd do it. I know she would. She always said that men were beasts and almost accepted the lustful side of their nature. And "St. Francis" is the patron saint of beasts, right? So his hospital would be an okay setting for a rendezvous. Right?

Darlene can get horny herself, not as often as me, but she has been known to pursue me and even rip my clothes off and have her way with me. Of course she's usually drunk when that happens. But she's a cheap drunk. Two or three glasses of rosé and she's a tigress in the bedroom.

Who am I kidding? I can't just go to Darlene's room and hop on. That would be rape. Would that be rape? Is it rape if the person would enjoy the sex, but is not awake enough to say outright, "Honey, let's do it!"?

Maybe I could try to wake her up first. She needs to get out of that coma. Come on, that can't be good for you, not as long as Darlene's been in hers. It's been weeks and weeks now. "Darlene, it's me," I'll whisper. Her eyes will open, and she'll whisper back, "I've been waiting for you."

And then we'll Do It. And if she needs to, she can go back into her coma afterwards. I'm usually practically in a coma myself afterwards.

Something tells me there is something wrong with this plan. But what is it?

What if I go there and Darlene wakes up in the middle of it and starts screaming?

That can't be good.

What if I can't get it up because I'm too nervous?

Naw, I'm never that nervous!

What if somebody comes in and catches me on top of Darlene? Those nurses might not understand.

What if I got underneath Darlene so that she's on top? She's a little bit hefty just normally. I might not be able to lift her when she's dead weight.

What if I just shoot on her? She's had me do that a few times. She didn't really like it, but she let me do it on my birthday.

Where should I shoot on her?

On her face?

In her mouth?

Oh, that's gross, if she's not into it. And she's never been that into using her mouth at the best of times.

She likes me using MY mouth, however. What a double standard!

Maybe I could put my thing in her hand? That would be less gross, wouldn't it? She'd didn't object to a hand job now and then. I'd clean it up. I promise!

But that IV in her arm is creepy.

What if I shot on her breasts? I mean on that blanket over her breasts? I wouldn't actually expose her breasts and then shoot on them! Jesus, what do you take me for?!

Of course she did like me playing with her breasts. She has nice ones. Substantial ones.

How about on her belly? On the blanket where her belly is, I mean. That's pretty tame. We've done that before, just rubbing bellies until I came. Darlene said it was "kinda adolescent," but it seemed pretty sexy to me. She must have had a hotter adolescence than I did!

But the blanket would get all wet! Yuck!

Oh, my God, what if I actually put it in her You Know What? I'd ask her permission and thank her profusely, before and after, like Native Americans do when they kill a buffalo or something. Right?

Maybe I really am a necrophiliac! (with good manners)

No, I know I'm not because if I did that I'd feel terrible after I came. I bet a necrophiliac doesn't.

What is a horny, healthy guy with a girlfriend in a coma supposed to do?

What if I started to do it, and there was some semen already there?! Oh, my God, what kind of hellhole is that St. Francis Hospital?!

Hey! Hey! I didn't do any of this stuff to poor Darlene. It's just a guy thinking aloud, for God's sake. I'm not going to do any of it. What do you take me for, a perv?

You take almost anybody and read their mind and I bet you'd find a perv.

⁂

You see your share of drag queens in San Francisco. Just not as many as most outsiders think. Some are very good at passing as women. Those are your trans-sexuals. They don't want to call attention to themselves. But your average drag queen is all about showing off. You know there's a man underneath the make-up and the eyelashes and the fancy dresses, and you know in your gut that you never, never want to actually engage in a fistfight with one because they'd probably whip your ass! Most of them have learned to be quite mouthy, no doubt because they have gotten flak from the mouthy Normal People. Please note: some of these Normal

People are wearing paint all over their own faces, only it's Raiders' football paint or the like. I especially noticed this when I went on those two dates with the man-nun. Lots of cat-calls and ugly name-calling – and the Bay Area is supposedly so LIBERAL.

My point is that I don't usually bother talking to drag queens when I'm working. Today was different. I guess I was feeling a little guilty about wanting to have sex with my girlfriend in her coma. Or perhaps it was because I had gotten a splinter in my thumb and it was making handling the cable car levers harder than usual. I had picked at the splinter, besides, and now my thumb was smarting. I thought I could distract myself until lunchtime.

So I turned a little to address this statuesque forty-something "gal" in platform shoes, beehive hair-do, and a ball gown from 1948 who was standing by herself holding onto a strap. "Getting much?" I asked.

She ignored me.

"Love your dress."

"I didn't wear it for you."

"Why do you want to wear a dress?" I knew it was a fatuous question, but my thumb was hurting. And did I mention that my girlfriend is in a coma?

"I am an entertainer!" she said grandly.

"I'm sure you are," I said. "Why do you think people get such a kick out of seeing a man wearing a dress?"

"You mean when they're not chasing us with a baseball bat?"

"Must be tough sometimes."

"I made my bed."

"Ever actually been hit with a baseball bat?"

"Not yet." She held up crossed fingers, much be-ringed fingers.

"Some people threaten us cable car drivers."

She did not respond.

"Gangs are on the cars now. I found a turd on the floor as well."

Still no response.

"People can be real shits, can't they?"

The drag queen gave me a sharp stare. "I don't care for this negativity."

"Negativity? I'm just sharing what happens sometimes."

"One cannot let unfortunate experiences govern one's reactions. It is always best to look on the bright side."

"The bright side of a baseball bat?"

"I refuse to be dragged down into the mud of a lower consciousness."

"Shirley, you jest!" I joked.

"I have learned not to surround myself with bitchiness or carping or complaining."

"You must spend a lot of time alone," I said.

"I am trying to reform the drag community and what I see as a terrible stereotype."

"Don't you think a little bitching clears the air?"

"No, I do not. I believe one should convert the unsavory into the uplifting."

I turned a bit more to savor this odd person. "I've read that shrinks say it's best to vent, not hold it in."

"In my experience, it becomes a life style – a life style I choose not to allow to bring me down."

"Well, I suppose some folks can overdo the complaining." Was that me? I wondered.

"They most certainly do." She drew herself up, quite huffy with self-righteousness, a sort of dowager drag queen of royal blood.

"Surely, you get together and dish?" I persisted.

"I leave that for others. I'd rather dine by myself than sit through a lot of catty, bitter commentary by people with vicious tongues."

"What do you think about global warming then?"

"I'm sure I don't know. I just try to entertain at my club and then get away from that scene as fast as I possibly can."

Yeah, it sounded sort of lonely, but I didn't say that.

"In case you think I am lonely, let me assure you that I am not. I am working on a musical about my life. I am three-fourths finished."

"How fabulous!" I said. I held back on "Is it any good?!"

"I am dedicating the musical to the memory of my late sister. "She was the most beautiful person in my entire life. She loved me even when she caught me trying on dresses as a boy. I am blending her rich, spiritual life in yoga and mine in the drag world in my musical."

"Really? I'd like to hear it." (I didn't really want to hear it.)

"Oh, it will be not for the masses but for a small, select clientele."

"*La Cage Aux Folles* was a big hit! Maybe yours will be too." (I was trying my best to be POSITIVE.)

"Oh, my musical will be much more elevated than that! The audience was laughing at drag in that monstrosity! But not in mine!"

"Tsk, tsk!" I said, waving my finger. "That sounds a trifle negative to me."

"Then it must be your influence, sir," she snapped. And with that my Militant Pollyanna moved to the rear of the cable car and avoided my negative aura like the plague it was.

What the hell is going on with the world when drag queens think they're holier than thou!?

ഗ ഇ

Uh oh!

There was an accident on a cable car this morning. Luckily for me it was not my car. Or I should say that I was off today. I took the day off because of some sniffles that I was worried might turn into something worse. I was supposed to have that shift, so I escaped. Seven people were injured when the car ran into a screw caught in the tracks and came to a sharp stop near Washington Street. It was raining then and hard to see. An ancient Asian man was thrown off and hurt his head on the street. The rest will have stiff necks most likely, but their injuries are not life threatening.

There are rumors that somebody deliberately put that screw in the tracks. It doesn't take that much to fuck up a line. Probably done by some trust-fund anarchist. "Screw you, cable cars, relics of the corporate past!" Call me old-fashioned, but I think anarchists should be tied to the cable car tracks and run over until they suffocate or be-shit themselves, or both. Anarchists, my ass! You think people are going to behave well then? They don't behave well now!

Or it could have been a taxi driver. They'd get more business if the cable cars went under. And they drive like maniacs and probably spew screws and other junk into the tracks.

Now I know who did it – those bicyclists! Some goddamned anarchist taxi-driver bike-riders did it, as I live and breathe!

(Am I getting paranoid?. . . Or just old?)

Already some loudmouth member of the Board of Supervisors has been saying, "Maybe it's time for the cable cars to go the way of the horse and buggy!" People were aghast. But maybe he's on to something, the passing of an era?

Had my cell phone stolen today, grabbed right out of my hand as I was calling the hospital to see how Darlene is. Naturally I can't identify the thief, BECAUSE THAT WOULD BE RACIAL PROFILING. Let's just say he was about twenty, tall, skinny, and NOT ASIAN and NOT WHITE. God, it fries my ass when you can't use your own observations about who commits crimes, even when you are the victim of the crime and it's your own cell phone that's stolen. I didn't report the theft. It wouldn't make any difference. People need to stop calling unpleasant facts about blacks "racism" and quit being such mealy-mouthed cowards. No wonder the crimes don't stop! Stop the denial! I'm not saying that *all* blacks are bad. In my experience, they vary from great to annoying to deadly. Cal Hutchins, one of the conductors, is a very personable guy, full of corny jokes. He's also black. He has a second job as a taxi driver at night, to pay child support. He tells me that he won't pick up black men, either. So does that make him a racist or a realist? I want other people to quit telling me what I see and what I don't.

I tell passengers not to sit there with their "smart" phones dangling in the air, ripe for snatching by Unknown Criminals, including black victims of course. They all seem more infatuated with Angry Birds and "apps" than their own safety. One guy today scolded me for interrupting his business call.

"Just trying to protect you, sir," I said in my best "professional" voice.

But then I saw a way to do better than that. Let me explain.

There are these two black con artists that ride on my car from time to time. They get on separately, two blocks apart, and then one of them starts fiddling with what are known as Cups and Balls, placing a little rubber ball under one of three cups and moving them around on a small board he puts on his lap. Naturally, most people watch him (unless they are on their cell phones!), and the first con man asks them if they want to guess – for money, this is. Everybody says no. Then the second con man gets on, and before you know it, he is asked to play by the first man. Now he agrees, and they set $20 as the bet. A ball is placed under a cup, hands shift the three cups around, the second guy guesses wrong and loses his twenty dollars. The secret of the con is that the second con picks a cup that is obviously *wrong*, and everyone watching can tell that it's wrong. So, you see, the other passengers think they are smarter than the poor loser, who now gets off the cable car.

Before you know it, someone else is betting against the guy with the cups. And guess what! Suddenly this guy is a whole lot faster and better, and he has another twenty dollars in his hand. "One more!" the con artist invariably says, and the sucker will bite. If they don't, the con artist says, "I give you twenty for a ten!" He smiles like the viper he is. Usually he walks away with all the cash the sucker has on him. If he's a tourist, it's usually a lot.

On this particular day, I glance back at Mr. Smart-Ass Smart Phone (who just happens to be white) and who had scolded me earlier as he sees the first part of the con, the obviously wrong guess and decides to get in on the action. "That sounds like a deal," he blurts out and looks toward me for confirmation. I should be watching the tracks better, to avoid an accident, but I cannot resist. I may not have larceny in my heart, but I do hold grudges. "Do you know this guy? Is he legit?" he goes on. He looked like a financial district type: expensive suit, wide yellow tie, shiny black shoes, clean shaven, and ready to sell your grandma on the stock exchange if it would earn him a quarter of a cent profit. (Not to *profile*, of course!)

"So far as I know he's legit," I say. (Yeah, a legit con man, asshole!)

So Mr. Smarty Phone Pants gets out his wallet, from inside his suit jacket, natch, not his back pocket, and he says to Cups and Balls Guy, "I'll bet you this hundred for those three twenties you've got." Well, isn't he brave!?

The con man hesitates for just a second, probably a part of his ploy. "You afraid?" Mr. Financial District gloats. His mother probably told him to Go for His Dreams!

The con man then takes out four more twenties and now holds seven of them up for all to see. "One hundred forty against your measly hundred!"

"So you'll give me a hundred and forty dollars if I guess the correct ball?" The Suit is just clarifying the verbal contract.

"Come on, man. You afraid? Your eyes no good?"

The Suit's eyes narrow and he gives a smile that's as wicked as his opponent's. He reaches into his wallet and takes out two more hundred dollar bills and fans out the three hundred dollars. "My eyes are so good I'm willing to bet my three hundred against your one hundred and forty." I'll out-macho your macho!

We're all watching this like fight fans now, of course. To hell with safety! I'm convinced several people skipped their stops just to see how it ended: Financial District versus Ghetto.

The Suit had pissed off the con man with that business bravado and takes more big bills out of his stash and now holds up his money. "One thousand dollars!" Ghetto announces.

The Suit blinks a bit. "Let's make it two out of three."

"You want to win two out of three?" the con man says.

"I want another chance if I lose the first time."

"Oh, okay. My English ain't so good." Again with the phony smile.

I'm almost tempted to warn Smarty Suit that he's going to lose and stop the whole game when Smarty takes out more dollars from another wallet on the other side of his jacket. "Tell you what. I will put up two thousand three hundred dollars if you'll put up three thousand dollars!" Ah, the shark turns!

"You try to take my hard-earned money?" the con man says.

"It's up to you," says Smarty Suit.

"You're on, brother!"

Down go the cups onto the little lap board. Inside one of the cups goes the ball. "You ready?" asks the con man. *Ax* the con man? (Oh, get over yourself!)

"Ready!" is the reply.

There's a swirl of hands; back and forth go the cups.

Then the cops raided us and we all went to jail for illegal gambling!

Gotcha! Didn't happen.

Smarty Suit suddenly gets all indecisive and his pointing finger moves from one cup to the next – and he can't make up his mind. People are calling out what they think is the right cup. Even I said, "The cup in the middle! The cup in the middle!" I had no idea which cup was the right one!

Sure enough, Smarty Suit picked the wrong one, the one to his left. He demanded to see where the ball was. It was under the one to his right. So I would have been wrong too. The difference is I didn't lose $2300!

Mr. Smarty-Ass Suit seemed stunned that he was wrong and had lost all that money to a street con man. "You should hire him," I advised. "He'll fit right into your firm."

So you see, I hate white businessmen criminals too! Like most things in life, that duel was not between the Good and the Bad, just between two different kinds of asshole.

I need a touching story about now. I know full well that most people love touching stories, even when they deny they do. They enjoy blubbering all over themselves, sucking up tears, chests heaving.

It was original intention to tell heart-warming tales of the wondrous cable cars and the loveable folks who ride them. The Chamber of Commerce wants me to! Folks dreaming of some mythical City by the Bay want me to. Even *I* want me to!

However, my experiences do not warrant such emotions. I wish the people I encounter daily now in San Francisco were better than they are. But the truth is diversity is a bitch and San Francisco has become a second-rate city, dirty and crime-ridden, especially downtown. Makes for different kinds of food, yes, but it also makes for the fact that the customs and values of the newcomers, who have come in such huge numbers, have superimposed themselves on Old San Francisco: such as being ethnic before being American, bribery as a way of life, not paying taxes when they have Cash Only businesses, patriarchy, sexism, homophobia, racism (between the various ethnic groups competing with each other for turf and power), superstitions (feng shui, head scarves on women, crossing themselves before every pitch, bathing in the filthy Ganges to "purify" themselves. (Okay, maybe not that last one!) Plus cruelty toward animals, particularly animals for food). Do you know you have to report a death in your house if you want to sell it now?

I have a cleaning lady who comes every couple of weeks to clean my condo. She says she's from Guatemala, but I bet it's Mexico. I pay her a fair wage – she agreed. Now she takes off early, as much as half an hour every time, and I'm afraid to confront her about it, because that would make me the Evil White Oppressor and even possibly make me lose the cleaning lady and her Mexican work ethic. Yeah, I know I can clean it myself, but I pay her to do it. She's grumpier than I am. I'm sure she is tired of cleaning other people's shit, but she's hardly "lovable." I think she'd cut my throat and take over my condo if she could get away with it. I'm not saying America was saintly or perfect previously. Hardly. But it was different, and I liked it more. It is changing right before my eyes. Sometimes I feel that History is stepping on my face, and I don't know how to cope with it.

Now where was that touching story I was going to tell?

Oh, I just remembered one.

There is this lady from Papua New Guinea who wears a hoodie and dark sunglasses when she rides my cable car. She is a sorceress. How do I know this? Because she told me so herself. The hoodie and dark glasses are out of fear that some of her countrymen have followed her here and are planning to torture and burn her to death. She always looks terrified, constantly glancing around. Apparently she put a spell on somebody's sister back in her Old Country, and the girl developed blisters in her private parts. That meant she couldn't get married. The relatives of the blistered girl set out to reek? wreck? revenge. They have followed the sorceress here to Baghdad by the Bay, and when they catch her . . . Could I make this stuff up?

What's the touching part?

Well, today three who looked like they might be from Papua New Guinea were hassling the sorceress at the rear of the car. Ralph Delfino, my conductor, who won't do diddly since he had open-heart surgery three months ago, wouldn't interfere in the hassling. So I did. So did two other Hispanic guys wearing hairnets and baggy clothes. (I don't think they were gay, despite the hairnets.) They were just about to "escort" the sorceress off the cable car and into God knows what torture chamber in some Tenderloin SRO when we good guys confronted the nasty revenge squad and threatened to have them arrested if they didn't desist.

I would have threatened deportation too, but that didn't seem likely in my town even if they started torturing her right there on the cable car! There was a lot of yelling and screaming in whatever language they speak in Papua New Guinea, and the woman rushed over and hid behind me. I think she even threw in a couple of new curses for each of her pursuers. I was hoping they might turn into pigs or something, but they didn't. They did look very annoyed.

"What the fuck's wrong with you shit-heads?" I screamed. "Leave your goddamned baggage back where you came from when you are in this country! We have enough baggage of our own!"

I'm sure they didn't understand a word of English, but they did seem to understand that I was trying to convince them they had to forgive the sorceress for the blisters and reconcile their differences. Of course they agreed and hurried away.

I wish I'd had a hand gun so that I could have finished them off and saved both the sorceress and me a lot of grief in the future. I knew that I was going on their Torture Shit List even as I preached to them about "religious liberty" and "the fucking US Constitution."

What's the uplifting part?

Later they found the sorceress and shot her twice, in the throat and arm, but she didn't die, and she got the gun away from them and shot them all in the head and they became very annoyed and dead. All parties learned the beauty of the Second Amendment, of the right to bare arms. (yeah, pun intended!) God Bless America!

If that's not touching and uplifting, I don't know what is.

ოყ ၆ი

Okay, let me try again. It didn't happen directly on a cable car, so does that still count? I wouldn't want to cheat you since you bought this book. You did buy it, right? I hope somebody didn't just leave it on a bus or something and you picked it up. Wow. I write the kind of book people leave behind on cable cars!

I saw Darlene again today, at the hospital. She looked very peaceful, although there was an eye booger near her left eye. I removed it with a Kleenex. Darlene seemed to have lost some weight. I couldn't tell if that was a good thing or not. Her breathing was normal, and I checked with the doctor to make sure Darlene's medical insurance was still good. It was. The last thing we needed was a stack of bills when she got out. (Let's face it, America sucks when it comes to medical bills!) I stood close to the bed with the doctor and asked if Darlene would ever come out of her coma.

"She will," the doctor said encouragingly. He was overweight, blotchy-skinned, short of breath, wearing thick glasses, and frazzled with having to be in another department in thirty seconds. But I still took hope from his words, both of them.

"What does she have exactly?"

He muttered some Latin name that I didn't quite catch. It sounded horrible. "We're just letting her body recover as slowly as it needs to. I've got to go."

"Well, thank you, Doctor," I managed.

"Talk to Darlene. It can only help."

"What if I call my friend the sorceress?" I said.

Either he didn't hear me or didn't have time, or didn't really care. Away he went!

"Do you want me to call the sorceress?" I asked Darlene, as a joke.

"Yes!" she replied, quite loudly.

So I called in the Papua New Guinean sorceress, and that holy woman cured my beloved Darlene of her malady, even the medically induced coma, and we all lived happily ever after in a culturally Diverse and Prosperous Land of Plenty. Amen. True story!

You don't believe me?

What REALLY happened is that a little girl about four years old, dressed in her hospital gown and bunny slippers, was wandering the halls of the hospital, unsupervised and no doubt illegally, and happened by Darlene's room. She peeked around the edge of the doorway, as cute as she could be, rather shy. Her head was shaven. She probably had leukemia or some other form of childhood cancer. "Hi," she said to me.

"Hi," I said back.

"Is that your wife?"

I started to clarify that Darlene and I weren't exactly married and a bit estranged, but something made me hold my tongue. "Yes, she's my wife," I said.

"She's pretty," the little girl said.

"Yes, she is."

"I'd like to be that pretty someday."

"I'm sure you will be," I said. "Maybe even prettier." The little girl was already cute.

The little girl shook her head. "Oh, I don't think so.

I will die before I'm five."

"Oh, no, you won't!" I protested, aghast.

"My brother told me I would. He's seven, so he knows. He said he heard our mommy say so on the phone to Aunt Mirosol."

"I'm sure your brother was just teasing you," I insisted. "We all know how mean brothers can be."

The little girl cocked her head and stared at me for a moment. "It's okay, Mister. I'm not afraid. Because if I die, then I'll be in Heaven with Saucy Boy, my cat." And then she literally skipped out of the room.

Yes, I admit it. I cried and cried like a baby, as I stood there looking at my Darlene with the "gypsy blood" who had given me a pet rat and seemed rested and happy only because she was in a coma and couldn't see the future.

CB BO

A raven landed on my cable car this morning. No, it did not quoth "Nevermore!" But it might as well have.

I think it might be an omen of things to come. I am not usually superstitious, but this raven was nasty-looking.

Its feathers were the color of the coals of Hell! Its mean, sharp beak kept pecking at a railing of the cable car. And those wicked eyes with those glistening bullets inside – you just know those ravens would savage your face and eat your teeth if they could.

I've seen them before, usually during the early shift. They get more cautious as the day wears on. You can still see them occasionally, high up on lamp posts or the eaves of buildings. I saw two of them pecking a pigeon to death once. I swear it. And another time one had a baby bird in its mouth, another species' baby! So I do not mess with ravens.

They are always hungry. Sometimes passengers will throw their left-over snacks or potato chips or half a sandwich to the birds who follow us. Sparrows and gulls have discovered that they can get freebies if they time it right. But they stay away from the ravens, because the ravens are the biggest bullies on the block. And these ravens don't look like fake, stuffed ones from a bad movie. They are alive and rapacious and threatening. If there is reincarnation, I want to come back as a raven.

Which brings me to the homeless man. He likes to ride the cable cars, but he doesn't like to pay. He probably makes more than I do begging, but he won't pay, no matter how much the conductors insist. They have pretty much given up on getting blood out of a stone.

He is in his sixties, I'd guess, or thirty going on sixty-five, from the hard life: hard drugs and lots of cheap wine. His nose looks like a rose, a rose with a bug growing inside it, and he is way wacky and talks to himself. He wears a long-out-of-fashion ankle-length black coat that was cheap when it was new and now looks like it has a sheen, a patina, on it. I doubt that he wears anything else under it. He likes to masturbate on the cable car too. He'll find a pretty girl and sit next to her, and before you can say boo, he's rubbing inside his coat pocket. She doesn't even have to be that pretty. A few women have complained about it. Most just get up and move away. Some don't seem to notice, preoccupied with their iPads and their iPods and their camera phones and what have you.

I'd hate to see the inside of his coat! One of these days somebody is going to snap his picture as he whacks off. But he'll just be back in a few days. You can tell when he does it because he gets this "ecstatic" look on his face for a few seconds when he Sees the Light. He doesn't make any noise, so that's a blessing at least. What I really hate about him is that he's getting more than I am!

So how do the ravens fit in with the homeless man? He doesn't like them. He tries to shoo them away. Naturally, they don't like him either. They try to shoo him away. I saw one raven almost land on the guy's homeless head. I'm positive he drew a little blood. "You ought to do something about them ravens!" he'll say to me.

"They're my police force," I say back to him.

"Fucking police!" he answers.

I agree. I hate the cops – unless somebody is vandalizing my car! Then they're not so bad. (If you want help committing suicide, just pick up a screw driver and call a cop.)

Last time I said to the guy, "Those ravens know what you're doing inside your coat pocket. Do you know that?"

The homeless guy snaps his head at me. "What are you jabbering about?"

I lowered my voice so as not to offend the other passengers. "The ravens know that you are . . ."I subtly shook my hand up and down a little to illustrate the masturbation.

"I don't know what you're talking about." He turned his head away, downright haughty.

"You're not fooling me, Mister," I said.

"You must have a dirty mind," he replied.

"We all have our needs. Just don't do it on the cable cars." (in front of other people!)

"I have scabies," he informed me.

"Thank you for sharing!"

"I have to scratch myself sometimes. To be polite, I do it through my pockets."

"Why don't you de-louse somewhere else?"

"They won't let me into any of the shelters anymore."

"I don't believe you."

"They accuse me of jacking off there. But I'm just scratching!" He seemed quite incensed about it.

"Can't you take a shower somewhere? I'll even buy you some scabies medication to use in the shower."

"That's what they all say!"

"That's what they all say?!"

"Yeah, and then they fail to provide any medication. They just kick me out!"

"You'd think you'd get tired of scratching all the time."

"You willing to let me use your shower? Huh?" (He knew I wouldn't.)

"You might never leave my place!" I protested.

"I'd leave, and I'd take your collection of old lace with me."

"My what? . . . I don't have a collection of old lace!"

"Oh, I bet you do too! Yards and yards of old lace!"

So now I knew that I would have to kill the homeless man – he had discovered my deepest darkest secret!

"If I catch you jacking off or even scratching on my cable car again, I'm going to . . . I'm going to . . ."Shit, I couldn't think of anything real!

"You're going to what? Report me? Hah!" He sat back and flung his arms back on the railing.

"I'm going to sic the ravens on you." I pointed to the sky. "I know their special language."

The homeless guy was at least Paranoid Schizophrenic, on a good day, and he sat up straight and dropped his jaw at what I had said. "The ravens?"

"They hate your guts already. You know they do. A word from me and you're a dead man."

"You can really talk to the ravens?"

"Who do you think made them peck at your head?"

"That was you?"

"And that was just a taste of what's coming."

"I . . . don't . . . believe you." It was clear that he at least half-believed me.

I threw the words like the daggers they were: "I know where you sleep!"

"You don't!"

"Oh, yes, I do, and my ravens will seek you out in the middle of the night and pluck out your eyeballs and crap in your nose!" Of course I didn't know where he slept, but he didn't know that I didn't know.

"You wouldn't!" He seemed to be growing more paranoid by the second.

"If you're lucky, I'll ask them to pluck out your teeth too! No extra charge!"

"You're crazy!" He got up from his seat and moved further away from me.

"Ravens love human teeth. They can't get enough!" I was on a roll now.

Just then, quite by accident, a raven flew past the front of the cable car. "See! They are my minions!" (At least I think it was an accident!!!)

The homeless man saw the raven and screamed. "You are the Devil! You are the Devil himself!!" He was trying to get off, but I wouldn't stop the car.

I confess I laughed maniacally and saluted the raven as it flew off. "Come back tonight, my dark bird friend, and I will tell you where to find this wicked man as he sleeps. And you and your flock can peck the scabies from his living flesh until you are satisfied and he is lifeless!" I pointed for all I was worth.

Yes, it was perhaps a bit extreme, but it got the scabies-laden "homeless" masturbator off my cable car. The ravens, not so much. They haven't obeyed a single order of mine since.

ଓ ଛ

It used to be just on a night when the fog blows in from the Pacific and swirls around, obscuring one's vision. I'm talking about the thieves who are stealing copper or any other kind of saleable wiring on the cable cars. These A-holes don't care who they inconvenience just as long as they can gut our wiring and sell it to some junk yard creeps who turn a blind eye to what they are buying. Now they are doing it in the daytime!

It was right after lunch today when I happened to look around and caught a glimpse of two males dressed in MUNI Repairs outfits. Now I don't know everybody who works for MUNI or even for the cable car division, but I did not recognize these two guys whatsoever. They also seemed a bit nervous. At first I assume my conductor for the day, Lester Ruiz, had spoken with them and said it was okay to check out the wiring at the rear of the cable car. He must have assumed the same thing about me. Usually they make repairs at night except in an emergency, like when we had that screw caught in the tracks. It may have been their first attempt on a cable car with real MUNI personnel onboard, which caused them to look less confident. Have you noticed how people can get away with murder if they just manage to look cool while committing a crime?

Both these guys were on the small side, in their thirties, I'd say. Maybe they'd stolen the MUNI repairmen uniforms. Maybe they had made them. I did a double take. They were actually cutting wires with these big shears they were carrying. One did the cutting, while the other stuffed the cuttings into a cardboard box. In fact, they had brought along three cardboard boxes in anticipation. What gall!

Suddenly I was filled with rage. Who did they think they were? It was just one more kick in the heart of San Francisco. Ruin the cable cars. What the hell did they care, as long as they got their lousy hundred bucks from the junk yard! Everything great about the city was being destroyed by A-holes! You can't go up on Twin Peaks any longer to catch the fantastic view from up there. You'll be hassled by teenage toughs, protecting "their territory." You can't go to the Castro Halloween street party anymore, because it got cancelled, and not because of the drag queens — because of teenage toughs from outside the city coming in to make trouble for the sheer hell of it. Complete with gunfire and several killings. And San Franciscans are so fucking P.C. they just let their city be taken from them. They wouldn't want to hurt anybody "feelings." Even the goddamned graffiti "artists" are excused because they "have nowhere else to display their urban art." The lowbrows drive out the few cheap, simple pleasures in life. It's not right, and I am not going to let it happen without a fight. If San Francisco is my turf, and it is, then GET THE FUCK OFF MY LAWN.

I wish I could say that I jumped on the wiring thieves and strangled them until their eyes popped out of their skulls. Only I didn't.

I did ask them for their IDs. They had some too. Probably fake. I didn't have any way of checking to see if they were legitimate or not.

Then they started ragging on me, saying, "We are here to check that this wiring meets the proper standards of the Americans with Disabilities Act!"

"What?!" I said with utter disbelief.

"If it is not up to snuff, we are going to shut you down."

Naturally, I became paralyzed with fear. The Americans with Disabilities people are ruthless! It did not get any more Politically Correct than that. So they knew they had my number. These guys were lying, no doubt. But I couldn't have been more intimidated unless they had said they were Veterans of the War in Afghanistan trying out their arm and leg prostheses by working on the cable cars!

Fuck it, I talk big, but I'm just as big a pussy as other people are.

⋘ ⋙

Now the "authorities" want to put spy cameras on the cable cars. To prevent "quality of life" crimes. I'm torn. On the one hand, we have had some serious shootings, thefts, and vandalism on the cars. Did I even mention the vandalism to you? Quite often somebody or somebodies sneak into the MUNI lots and spray paint their stupid tags. They used to spare the cable cars. Not anymore. They are often in any language but English. And, no, I wouldn't like them any better in English. (Press #1 to read graffiti tags in English!) They're usually about La Raza or Central American or Filipino political issues or other crap I don't want to hear about. These guys won't be happy until they make the United States as shitty as the shit holes you came from? No, thank you. Why do people keep insisting that I see how wonderful Diversity is? A lot of Diversity is downright awful, not an improvement. If I want graffiti in a foreign language, I'll travel! Travel is supposed to be broadening. I have found it usually makes me want to hurry back home. And now home isn't even home anymore!

As for the spy cameras, maybe they'll stop some of the crime, but maybe they'll just catch me getting that one blow job. Or with Bitty the Second, my pet rat. Headline: MUNI Employee Makes Poor Rat Smell Armpit. Or: MUNI Employee Has Unnatural Relationship with Rat. Or maybe they'll catch me picking my nose. I've also been known to take a leak in a plastic cup on a cable car when nobody can see me, late at night, or when one of our restrooms is inadvertently locked. Howls will go up. Fire that gripman! He pissed! You can actually see a PENIS if you blow up the video! Yeah, yeah, my penis is not what it used to be, I suppose, but I can still fit it over a plastic cup to take a leak. God knows, how hard it is to find a public toilet in San Francisco. You have to buy a three-course meal or give up your first-born son to get past the RESTROOMS FOR EMPLOYEES ONLY signs.

What else do I want kept private? Probably most of the stories I've told you already. What if people knew they were being videotaped? They might hesitate to do the very things that make the stories "interesting." Not much story value in saying "people behaved admirably all day today." This is what is called a "paradox," I think. Finally I understand what Mrs. Digbee, my tenth-grade English teacher, was trying to explain to us.

Another paradox is that the stories that happen more and more are what are killing the cable cars and may lead to their total departure from the streets of San Francisco. Or into a dusty, old museum, like the stagecoach or the Model-T. It is also what makes them "interesting."

Why is everything so complicated? It didn't used to be. . . Did it?

ભ છ

I went to visit Darlene after work today. She's still in a coma. But a male nurse mentioned that he had seen her open her eyes two days ago. "For how long?" I asked him. "Oh, just a few seconds." I guess I was supposed to take that as progress.

I looked down at Darlene. She did look rested. Only it wasn't a good kind of rested. Her body seemed deflated somehow. Her color was too pale.

Guess the hospital was overcrowded because there was a rack with a large x-ray on it that had obviously been pushed into Darlene's room in a corner. In the X-ray was the clear outline of a razor blade. Somebody must have swallowed it, right? You don't accidentally wind up with a razor blade in your gut, do you?

I felt that I ought to say some things out loud to Darlene, something kind. I read somewhere that even in comas, people can hear things. At the same time I was afraid that others would overhear me. I don't like to get all gushy in public. Also, what I wanted to say to Darlene wasn't completely gushy.

So I looked directly at her and sent her my thoughts:

I'm sorry if I haven't been a good boyfriend. I realize that I should come here every day, and I haven't. On the other hand, are we even a couple anymore? We've been growing apart for some time. Your coma just sort of cements the deal, wouldn't you say? If you could say. Maybe you don't even want me to come here.

Are you lonely in here? I hope that you are not awake right now, aware of me, of everything, but unable to move. I would truly, truly hate that. Much better to be in a fog.

I'm pretty lonely myself, and I'm not enjoying my job very much. People are getting on my nerves, which are frazzled enough because of your coma and my horniness and my awareness of growing older. I pulled a muscle in my upper belly today, and it's still making me wince. Those things used to go away almost immediately.

At least I'm not in a coma.

Maybe it would be better to be in a coma, you think?

But maybe, Darlene, if you woke up, we could get back together again. We'd fight most likely, but we'd make love too. I love going out to the Cliff House for dinner with you and watching the waves from the Pacific right outside the window. We'd look out at Seal Rock and feel all warm and toasty sitting inside, enjoying the food and each other. You'll have one Bloody Mary too many and getting sloppy when you talk – almost as if you were in a coma. . . Sorry.

We wouldn't have to say very much, and probably not a sentence of it would be earth-shaking or of any importance whatsoever to anyone else in the universe, just little reminiscences about things we've done together. Perhaps a loving look here or there with our mouths full. Probably a few digs thrown in too. You'd reach across the table and wipe some mustard from my chin. "Hey, keep your hands to yourself, lady!" I'd say, pretending to be mad, but secretly enjoying you touching me, caring enough to want me to look presentable.

We'd stroll outside the Cliff House and look down at the ruins of the Sutro Baths on the edge of the ocean, hoping for a glimpse of an otter or a water bird, and being satisfied with the cold wind and my arm around your shoulders and a sweet word or two whispered in your ear.

Please wake up, Darlene. Let us try again. Please.

My thoughts were interrupted by another group of interns and a senior doctor, this time a woman with a brusque demeanor, barging into Darlene's room. "There it is!" the woman doctor said, pointing at the x-ray attached to the wooden rack. The interns looked over at the razor blade. Then they looked at me, as if I had something to do with it. Then they looked back at Darlene. They didn't say anything, but they clearly thought it was her x-ray. I'm not sure what "askance" means, but I'm pretty sure they looked "askance" at me. No doubt *I* had shoved the razor blade down Darlene's throat!

I glared back at them and said, "She thought it was delicious!" And then I left and went home and ate a razor blade of my own. (That's a JOKE.)

CB EO

I wish I could say that Darlene woke up as I was leaving her hospital room, but that didn't happen. Maybe I should pray? I stopped praying in the fifth grade when I didn't get the roller skates I wanted so bad.

Some guy was praying on my cable car today. And I don't mean quietly to himself. I'd have no problem with that. But this guy was praying out loud, on his knees in the middle of the car. He was about fifty, black, portly, fat-faced, with a bow tie on. I'm not sure what set him off, or if he had just planned to come there and "pray on a San Francisco cable car." He lifted his arms up to God Above and started speaking in tongues. Maybe he was just having a stroke? Naw, he was speaking in tongues. I couldn't actually tell what he was saying, since I don't speak Tongues. It was rather showy and full of himself, I'll give him that.

I gather it had something to with San Francisco being the modern-day Sodom and Gomorrah. (I'd say it's more a modern-day Tower of Babel. And you know how well that went.) The guy did throw in a couple of "Save this wicked city!" prayers, along with "Or wipe it from the face of the Earth, as You have destroyed other evil places in the past!"

"Thou art disturbing the other passengers," I finally said to the Man of God.

"They need to be disturbed, for they are sinners!" he said back to me.

"Judge not lest ye be judged," said I.

"God is not mocked!" said he.

"I don't believe God gives a fuck." I knew better than to keep on quoting Scripture with this character.

The Man of God now got up off his knees and came closer to me, full of righteous wrath. He shook his holy finger right in my face. "I am here to witness to you. The Lord has asked me to save your soul."

"I don't want you to save my soul!" I replied. "In fact, I doubt that people even have souls."

The Man of God's eyes grew wide with disbelief at what I had just said. "You don't believe people have souls? That's the only thing about them that matters!" He literally placed his two hands over his ears and rocked back and forth. "Let this sinner hear Your message through me, Your vessel, O Lord!"

"You have a lot of nerve, you know that? And so does your Lord," I said.

"I am but the vanguard of an army of believers who are coming to save this wicked, wicked city from themselves!" he shouted.

"Oh, really? And where are you from?"

"Gary, Indiana."

"Save Gary, Indiana first. I hear it's a real hellhole."

"It is a righteous place! Glory hallelujah!"

"Exactly my point. I hear you are on everybody's bucket list. Your cable cars are especially noteworthy.

Probably even holy." God, I was enjoying being a smart-ass with this guy.

Then he grabbed me by the throat and forced me to endure water thrown on my head until I was SAVED. "We'll get you into a creek soon for the total immersion you need," the Man of God explained.

No, again I have lied about really happened. I knocked him down and pissed on his head until he was Born Again-Again. The piss seemed to bring him out of his religiously induced mania. Sopping wet, his shook his head, blinked, and started to weep. Kinky? It was no kinkier than what he was really doing to the rest of us.

Let me think now. What did I actually do to Holy Man? I called MUNI headquarters and had him removed by Security for disturbing the peace. God, could that Man of God swear a blue streak! He knew some curse words that I'd never even heard in the US army. Let alone God's Army.

No, I don't believe the way to "save" San Francisco from its many and undoubted frailties is through religious crackpots. That's even worse!

ଔ ଓ

The Mayor of San Francisco went riding on my cable car today. You would think that would be a good thing. He was there to show that "our cable cars are Safe, Sane, and Clean." That can only mean one thing: the cable cars are NOT safe, sane, and clean. The little mayor who came up with the slogan is of Korean ancestry, dapper in his tailored suits, with a speckled gray mustache, and a pushed-in nose that too often has a bit of nasal debris (shall we say) that glistens under the lights of the camera whenever he is interviewed on TV. Apparently no one has the nerve to tell him to keep his nose clean, in more ways than one.

He shook my hand. We had a photo "opportunity" near the grip. He rang the cable car bell with the conductor, Biff Spaulding, and everybody giggled about that. We rode up Powell Street as the Mayor waved and stood up, waved and stood up. There were five others as part of his contingent, carefully chosen to show the Diversity of the city. One of them was an ambisexual double amputee – at least. Various television stations had sent out crews to capture the historic ride to have for NEWS AT 10 or NEWS ALL NIGHT. Reporters from the traditional newspapers were there too. It was all very carefully planned as a media blitz to counter the bad publicity the cable cars have been getting for some time now.

A homeless man had been run over by a cable car a couple of weeks before the Mayor's ride. I was off that day, but it seems the poor fellow had been drunk or drugged, or both, and lay down on the tracks on Hyde Street under a cardboard box he used for shelter. He became a double amputee himself, although I don't think he was ambisexual. Two days later he died. And thus was spawned the Safe, Sane, and Clean campaign. I had no real objection to trying to save the cable cars. For one thing it would be saving my own job. I'm kinda doing the same thing in this book I'm writing, trying to prove the cable cars are marvelous and picturesque and a National Treasure, and all that. I'm just not sure my stories are doing that job! Maybe I'm helping to kill the cable cars forever!

The Mayor's Safe, Sane, and Clean ride was going pretty well, bringing back "the spirit that made San Francisco great," according to some flyers his staff handed out to all and sundry. But then six homeless men and one homeless woman boarded the same cable car around Post Street, together, as has become their wont. Their want? They had started out rather humble, one by one holding out their dirty begging cups and bedraggled hands begging for alms. At first they were relatively easy to control and shoo off the cars when each one was by himself. But as the years wore on, they learned to work as a pack, first three, then more. I've seen up to ten boarding at a time, grim-faced and adamant. One hand-written sign read: DONATE OR WE'LL EAT YOU. Or it might as well have! JESUS WANTS YOU TO LOVE YOUR NEIGHBOR was another sign. They were all "signs of the time," whatever they said. Those of us who actually worked on the cable cars had tried speeding up to avoid the Militant Beggars, but they had learned to outwit us by having some of them go on up ahead, get on, and help the others climb aboard even when we went fast. We had reported the problem, but nothing had been done, no doubt because of a paralysis about what to do from all sides.

So here was the little Mayor and his cronies being invaded by what I called the Pirates of Powell Street or, sometimes, the Homeless Hordes. Seven determined beggars with angry faces and sticks and canes can (and did) intimidate just about anybody. I saw one of the Mayor's contingent pull out a gun from her purse, but the others shushed her into putting it back. It would be a total disaster if they wound up shooting even one homeless person. (I'm sure I would have wept too, like a goddamned fucking baby!)

The Mayor stood up and began to make the most important speech of his life. "My friends, I appeal to you to put down your weapons. Let us see what we can do to end this problem on the streets of San Francisco.

If you will trust me, I promise that I will see that your needs are tended to just as soon as we are able!"

He went on, but the Pirates of Powell Street kidnapped the Mayor and got off near Pine Street. They held him for ransom, but nobody would pay the $20,525 they demanded. So, after a week, they let him go. He was founded disheveled and somewhat incoherent, wandering the streets. Everybody mistook the Mayor for just another homeless person, and so he was not identified for another whole week after that.

No arrests have been made. The Safe, Sane, and Clean campaign is, shall we say, now on hold.

C3 &0

There seem to be even *more* drunks on the cable cars lately. I am not sure why this is so. My suspicion is that some company is advertising Get Buzzed with Gus. How do I know this? Because I now see private busses pull up at Powell and Market and unload twenty to thirty people, most of them already half-buzzed. On the side of the bus it says GET BUZZED WITH GUS. Duh. They then get aboard a cable car, led by Gus, and seat themselves all high and mighty and start ordering drinks, which come out of boxed wine containers commandeered by Gus. Gus is a woman, by the way, tiny and feminine with a "piercing" through her nose. UGG! She seems to be about forty and wears big flowery hats. I think she is a front for some liquor company. Or maybe she has simply learned to exploit the fame of the cable cars. (Like me?) The difference is I'm trying to save them. She's just trying to make a profit.

The drunks are determined to have a jolly good time and whoop and holler until they are hoarse. They almost always spill their wine. Sometimes they toss it at each other and usually miss. I dutifully inform them that no alcohol is allowed on public transportation. They invariably say, "But it's the cable cars! Don't be a party pooper!" Gus gets right up in my face or the conductor's and says, "We have a permit for a wine tasting!" Then she flashes some vague piece of paper in seven languages which nobody can't read because she waves it so fast. They stay up to an hour, or until the boxed wine runs out. At least three people on every trip get sick and vomit, always on the seats. I'll look back and see them with their heads over the side of the cable car, puking their guts out. When they sit up, even with puke dribbling from their lips, they give me the Thumbs Up sign. Then they break into "Open your golden gate" or else "I Left My Heart in San Francisco," or both. The whole thing seems to be a growing trend. I think they're even flying in from North Dakota to Get Buzzed with Gus. I cannot seem to stop them. So maybe I should join them? WILD, DRUNK CABLE CAR DRIVER THRILLS LOCALS, TOURISTS ALIKE. I can see the headline in the *Chronicle*.

Ordinarily, I'd say the drunks don't do that much damage, except for the throw up and the wine stains, and it might even be becoming a new tradition, like the huge pillow fight on Valentine's Day in Justin Herman Plaza. Ordinarily, I'd say that. But yesterday the whole thing got a whole lot uglier.

About halfway through the "party," some gentleman with a tumor on his face got on board. I've seen the man now and again. He does his best to hide the tumor with a scarf around his neck and jaw, and he keeps his eyes down. I think he may be from India with the coloring to match as well as a certain formality to his body language. He's about fifty, slight of build, with bright, taking-it-all-in eyes. The drunks caught his attention, and he caught theirs. The wine had passed from the light-headed, giddy stage to the darker, meaner one, for at least half the drunks. "Hey! It's the Elephant Man!" one of them yelled out. "Hey, Elephant Man, have a drink with us!" Some cups of wine were proffered.

"I don't drink," Elephant Man said.

"Oh, too good for us, huh?!" the drunk said.

"No, thank you."

"You are going to have a drink with us, Elephant Man!" came the insistent reply.

"No, I am not!" came an even more insistent answer.

"It'll make you forget your troubles, dude." The drunk's eyes were already turning even meaner.

"I am not unhappy, sir," was the dignified reply.

"Well, you should be. I would be, if I looked like you."

"You are disgraceful and hideous drunks. You have made yourselves ugly deliberately. I, on the other hand, accept my tumor as a gift from the Universe."

"You must be joking. That ugly fucker covers up half your mouth."

"It is a gift!" Elephant Man therewith pulled away his scarf and defiantly revealed his whole tumor. It was a doozy. It was slightly lighter in color than his regular skin and looked like some sci fi creature feeding on the lower part of his face, pulling one side of his mouth off kilter. "Even with this, I am more beautiful than any of you revolting alcoholics!" he said with considerable pride and venom.

The party drunks took umbrage at this slur, including those who had just then registered the full hideousness of the man's deformity and were trying not to look appalled. On various faces you could see that they were torn between sympathy, disgust, and outrage that Elephant Man thought he was better than they were.

"It's rosé!" one of the drunks added pitifully. "And we're having a wine tasting, asshole!"

"You will not make me partake of your poisonous brews!"

"Hold him down!" one of the party winos yelled. "And I'll pour this wine down his disgusting mouth!"

Several drunks got up to do the deed. Some others were saying to leave the poor man alone. I thought about shutting down the cable car and kicking the entire lot of them off. But Elephant Man beat us to the punch. He jumped up and grabbed a box of wine from Gus's hands and tossed it underhand from the cable car. It landed with a juicy plop near the curb. Then he turned and headed for another box of wine on someone's lap. This time, however, the drunks were too fast for him, or too many. They wrestled him to the floor of the cable car and held him down. He screamed bloody murder (in Hindi, I think). Then Gus's assistant started pouring wine from a box onto the guy's deformed face. Most of it spilled onto the floor, causing some of the drunks to slip and slide. Some of the wine went down his throat.

I thought they'd stop, but somehow another box of wine appeared, and this time they pried open Elephant Man's mouth and filled him up with rosé, choking and coughing though he was. When he was good and drunk, they dropped him off the rear of the cable car. He was so loose now I don't think he broke any bones. They threatened to do the same to me unless I drove them back to where we'd started and without notifying the cops. Hey, I'm an agreeable sort!

They left me a hundred-dollar tip. No word yet from Elephant Man.

Don't you wish you were there?! Call Gus!

ଓ ଔ

Do you want to hear the story of the old lady with the Personal Problem? Of course you don't. She got on in the Tenderloin this afternoon. Do I look like a priest? She seemed to think I was her father confessor. She plopped her huddled mass right behind me, bigger than life. She was seventy-five, if she was a day. Red-face, broken teeth, probably terrible, sour breath, though she didn't get close enough to prove that. Is it just me, or are there ever more "marginal" people riding my cars these days? And they keep wanting to "share" their miseries with others, namely, in this case, me. I can give "good back" when I wish to, and I thought I was giving it to my confessee. Only she was not about to be ignored. "I'm Hot Mama. I think I'd make a great reality show," she said by way of introduction, shading her eyes with one hand against the severe San Francisco afternoon sun. "I'm a real housewife of the Tenderloin!" She laughed like a farm animal being slaughtered.

I didn't bite.

"I have a serious Personal Problem," she continued.

Me no hear.

"I bet you can't begin to guess what it is."

Speaka no English.

"It's medical."

Go and sin no more.

"I have had warning signs for months now, but today I finally learned what I have."

"Notice the lovely St. Francis Hotel to your left!"

I called out to all the passengers. Usually I don't act like a tour guide, but anything to throw Hot Mama off my trail.

I was wearing the cap with sunglasses attached that I use whenever the afternoon sun is particularly strong, and pulled it down, trying to see enough to drive the cable car and yet not be blinded by the light.

Hot Mama was not giving up. "It's the worst one he's ever seen. That's what the doc in that visiting ambulance whatchamaycallit told me."

"TMI," I said without turning around.

"What's that mean?" she said back.

"Too much information."

She paused, then said, "I thought we were living in the Information Age."

"Good one!" I managed. "I'm going to write a book called *The Too Much Information Age*. But will anybody buy it?!"

"That sun is real strong," she said, putting both hands above her eyes. "I wonder if I put that on my Personal Problem it would cure it."

What in the world???!!!

"That sun is like a beam from Heaven," she observed. "Maybe the Lord is telling me to allow that sun to cure my Personal Problem."

No, He isn't! (No, *She* isn't, either!)

The lady hadn't seemed that crazy when she'd gotten on. But things were not looking up. "If the sun is that bright, it must mean that the Lord's healing power is right there, above us, ready to be used when we are in trouble." She was doing a good job of convincing herself.

What next? Disrobing? Exposure of the Personal Problem to the assembled flock? Followed by a mass exodus from my cable car, including by me? "Lady!" I cried out, "Take it where the sun don't shine!"

"Well!" she said indignantly. She stood up and came up right behind me and slapped my neck, hard. "The driver on the last cable car was much nicer than you!" she informed me. "Let me off!"

Between her slap and that "golden sun," like in that song, I lost control of the grip for a few seconds and bumped into a baby carriage I couldn't see at a crosswalk. The baby was not injured whatsoever, but the mother was very upset and filed a complaint against me. Another complaint and I could be fired. Now I have a Personal Problem too.

☙ ❧

Some people are not going to like what I am about to say. That's even assuming you've liked anything up to this point. I feel all out of sorts of late. I have had a queasy stomach and a sore throat for a week. It doesn't get worse; it doesn't get better. Maybe if I had a girlfriend I would feel so cranky, at least a girlfriend who wasn't in a coma. I have no friends, no sex life (not even with myself), a job that I like less each day, and I don't like what is happening to my hometown, dear old San Francisco.

The worst part is that I am not permitted to lay blame on the plight of dear old San Francisco on anybody except Republicans. They are fair game for anything around here. However, I am not political. Lots of people are not political. We know we should be interested, but we simply aren't.

I try and try to think why I should be happy that San Francisco is so "diverse" now. The only one I can come up with is the value of my condo has gone up in value, quite a bit in fact, because people are clambering all over one another to buy property in my home town. Some of them are robber barons from You Know Where (Asia!). There are all sorts of financial schemes among family and business associates to beat the regular American system. They are thoroughly "racist" and "xenophobic" against other races and ethnicities and religions in their home countries and are here as well, except that you don't understand what they are saying in their languages.

The health care system is forced to take care of elderly grandmas imported from Hong Kong, along with their ivory collections. Social Security is paying disability for folks who barely paid a dime into the system. And I'm the bad guy for noticing? Not so.

It's not about color. That old crap. A few people of color are a charming diversion. (I noticed that I was that the time I went to Hong Kong for a week –I was the charming diversion.) It's about numbers. HUGE numbers. When the existing population is replaced by well over fifty percent, who then become rivals, it's not immigration. It's an INVASION. Yeah, yeah, we're all the children of immigrants. No, we're not. Some of us were born here, descendants of the Sky and the Waters. At least we don't have to "celebrate" being overwhelmed and driven out. (Peace to the Native Americans. Now I feel your pain.) (I want a casino for mine!) Besides, you lost. Grow a pair!

I can hear the sound of Progress stomping on my face!

I overheard a scary conversation on my run today. So what's new about that?" you ask.

What was most scary, besides the content, was the fact that the two people didn't feel the need to speak Arabic, or whatever it is they speak in Morocco, nor the need to keep their voices low. I also have excellent hearing. Maybe I'd be better off if I were deaf. Or deaf, dumb, and blind?

One of the two was what I'll call Mr. World Traveler. He wore Western clothes (a polo shirt and khakis) and had thinning hair and a confidence that seemed to say "I have a big dick."

He was talking to a young woman who might have been twenty or so. She had dark, pretty hair, large brown eyes, and seemed to be dressed in a restaurant's waitress outfit. I gathered they were both from Morocco but knew each other not from there but from here. He had been her customer at her restaurant. I think she was a Berber. Or maybe she said her father was a barber. They both had heavy accents. I've gotten pretty good at understanding foreign accents from all my passengers asking me things, but these two were challenging.

What started out as mere chitchat turned into a discussion of their mutual love of Islam. I guess they are not permitted to discuss their mutual contempt for Islam?! Mr. World Traveler bragged that he had visited 65 different countries and prayed in each one. The waitress said that she hoped to travel one day. He said that he was traveling so much because he was trying to get "refugees" from Libya and Syria and other Arab countries "embroiled in conflict" more visas to come to the United States. "Oh, that is so wonderful of you!" the waitress said. "We will see things improve in this Godless nation," Mr. World Traveler said, nodding approval of his own words.

"What?!" I swore, under my breath of course. He could say out loud that he wanted to bring tons of refugee Muslims to impose their "values" on me and my bi ways, but I had to secretively mumble my objection to his plan! Things are bad here, yeah, but their religion is about as far from the answer as I can imagine.

"I believe that we have an inside track in Washington," Mr. World Traveler bragged some more.

"How soon?" the waitress asked. "I feel so alone here sometimes. I would love to speak my own language again. Or maybe learn Syrian."

"Take a course!" I grumbled. I think they overheard me this time.

They didn't do a secret handshake or pass a spy note after that. They didn't have to. They gave me a superior look that said, "You want to pray five times a day. You know you do. And no more beer for you after work. And trans means DEATH. God is great!"

They got off and probably ran off and got married and started working on their NUMEROUS OFFSPRING right that minute.

Talk about Crusaders! But "San Francisco values" mean you have to turn a blind eye to the beliefs of these people, even defend them. Even when they're "moderate," they're to the right of the Nazi Party. Gays, Jews, and liberals will be the first to go! You can't quote me!

ɔ ʚ

Today somebody boarded my car near Leavenworth on crutches. I even helped him up since my woman conductor was busy in the back. He appeared to be from some land that permits alcohol. In fact, he was using up other folks' allotment of alcohol, to judge from the puffy-eyed, puffy-faced visage he presented to the world. I think he had some Asian, Malaysian, or Eurasian in him. You never used to see Asians drunk in public, not in San Francisco anyway. They were too proud or took care of their own, or something. But this character was a Free Spirit, not held back by shame or "family" or anything else, it seemed. Demon Drink had him in His vise! (Why does it have to be either No Alcohol at All or Face-on-the-Sidewalk-Dead-Drunk?! What about some moderation?!) He could not or would not speak English. I don't know what his language was – Advanced Drunk maybe?

So what does Puffy Face do once he's safely aboard? He lays his crutches across several seats and then pulls down his pants, exposing his buttocks immediately since he has no underwear on. He grabs hold of a pole on the side middle of the car and begins to act like he's a stripper in a strip joint. At first it was sort of funny. There he was mooning pedestrians and automobile drivers, gyrating in all his devilish drunken glee. (Hey, I've thought about doing it myself!) But then he starts flashing his dick too. He didn't seem to have much to flash with, but that didn't seem to bother him. Those of us inside the cable car had already seen the "flashing equipment" more than we'd wanted to. Now the rest of the world could see what they had been missing. Soon enough, every stitch of clothing was off and whirling in the air.

Eventually, my conductor, Petra, she who has no upper body strength at all, and I managed to get Puffy Face off the cable car and threw his smelly old clothes and crutches after him. He waved at us and did have enough English to say, "Me love America!"

This can't continue.

ог во

I got shot today. Don't ask!

When people argue about immigration, they always pick unlikely examples to prove their point. I am just going by the everyday examples I see. I think I can tell the foreign tourists from the undocumented stayers. As a matter of fact, I have been approached by ICE (Immigration and Customs Enforcement) to keep an eye out for such folks and report them. I am not a spy, however. It's too icky. "Hey, To Each His Own Up to a Point." "Live And Let Live." "Irritated Is Better Than Bored." (That last one is one I made up about my life.)

I don't want to have to spy to get people out of my hair. I just want to COMPLAIN about it. And I just want them to stop coming in such large quantities that they can't be assimilated, and don't really want to be assimilated.

I realize this is how history works. (I read a book once!) Tribes get too numerous for their own space and then spread out to space belonging to other tribes. Like the Vikings or the Mongols. Or the Mormons. They then all fight, flee, or fuck, often in some pretty horrific combinations, and then five hundred years go by and they put up a plaque that says: ON THIS DAY IN . . . Usually the plaque is so rusted or covered with dirt you can't read it.

It's a very messy "system," like making sausage. I just feel like I'm part of the sausage-making, as we speak.

Maybe if I was sexually attracted to Asians or Hispanics or even Russians, I'd welcome them with open arms. I suspect that is what's going on with people who would never admit it. "I want to fuck those slanty-eyed bitches with their legs up around my neck!" "*Latino* dick! Oh, Jose, plow it into me!" Isn't that the way people really carry on when they have sex, whether they say it out loud or not? You hear all this lovey-dovey crappola about "finding the one you love" and "the right to love whom you love." Please! Even the gays are using this sentimental shit to get the right to marry. I'd expect more from them. "I want

Scott to sit on my face until the end of time!" "Lulubelle loves my endless pubic hair and can't get enough!"

Politics quite often follows sex drive. Not always. (Often enough.) I don't know nothin' about Darwin's theory of the survival of the fittest, not exactly. But I do know when I'm being eaten alive.

Oh, did I mention that a sniper on top of a downtown building shot at my cable car today? I don't believe it was aimed at me personally, but it did wing me and killed Bitty the Second, my pet rat, with a bullet right, through his body on the rebound from mine.

They caught the guy, they think. He is from Yemen, over-staying on his student visa. Oh, I hate to STEREOTYPE people! I'm sure he's a devout Quaker.

 C3 &0

I had a little chat with my "superiors" at MUNI this morning, before my shift. I was surprisingly nervous, considering that I have quite good seniority. Ram Singh, who is a Sikh, said they were worried about me, that I may have used a "racial slur" when I was kicking the puffy-faced flashing drunk goon off my cable car. A "racial slur" is more important than "Thank you for getting that obnoxious slob off

MUNI"?! What is wrong with this picture? The worst part is that I had NOT used a "racial slur," no matter how tempted I might have been to do so. I know the realities of the changing universe around me. It is a strange, strange world in which even the hint of a "racial slur" trumps common sense. Ram Singh even seemed to hint at me retiring. He said there were some "bonus plans" being considered to "help with Diversity." When I objected, Ram Singh said, "People who aren't ethnic wouldn't understand." I am happy to say I answered back: "Ram, all people are ethnic. It's just seems that some are more ethnic than others."

It's just another form of Affirmative Action, which is still in place as a federal policy although we supposedly voted it out in California. If you want your racism, there it is: AFFIRMATIVE ACTION. It was signed into law by Richard M. Nixon, yet another blot on his character! It was supposed to work this way: if two people up for the same job, have the same qualifications, the job goes to the one in the Approved Categories List, to make up for past discrimination. The trouble is that it soon became – any person in the Approved List gets the job even when less qualified than the white male standing there with his dick hanging out (or shriveled up). People who have themselves never suffered a moment of discrimination suddenly are claiming positions they have no right to. I see it in who they hire to operate the cable cars. Some are fine. Some are incompetent, but, oh, they are "women" or "people of color." The quality of the cable cars has started to decline, but you can't speak up. You have free speech in America, unless you try to use it!

Well, call me "white shit" all you like. I am not going to be forced out of my job and give it to you! No job, no life. It's slightly more subtle, but it's still genocide. Believe me, I won't go like the Jews did.

Cᴙ ꙮ

I can hear you saying, "What happened to Good Old What's His Name and those wild, funny stories he was telling us about the cable cars? He's becoming a real downer."

You're right. Americans will tolerate anything except pessimism!

A funny thing did happen on the cable car three afternoons ago. Somebody left a satchel full of money behind when they got off. At first, I thought it might be a bomb, given my recent run-ins with the like and that sniper who winged me. I am still very stiff in the upper body – if not the lower! MUNI has agreed not to prosecute me for having a pet rat on my person, which is against the rules, because nobody but Bitty the Second was killed. Poor little rat, you did not die in vain. Maybe if I had actually been killed in the line of duty, I'd even get a Purple Heart in the Ethnic Wars of the 21st Century. (Or 72 virgins in Heaven who aren't in a coma!) Yuck, yuck, yuck.

Inside the satchel were bundles of US dollars in hundreds and twenties. I did not do a formal count, but it seemed to be over fifty thousand dollars. I didn't think the bills were marked with anything, such as a dye that explodes when you touch them. And nobody saw inside the satchel except me. Lars Pettigrew, my conductor, did see me checking it out and asked what was in it. He's one of the ones who steals fares from the fare box. I told him it was cat litter – used. Somehow he didn't want to see it! I suppose the money belongs to some drug dealer or some banker. So far, no one has asked about a satchel at Lost and Found. Believe me, I keep checking.

The bag of money is now under my bed at my condo. God, there's a lot of dust bunnies under there. I need to have the cleaning lady be a little more thorough. She intimidates me, though, because she is so sour. If I ask her to remove a cobweb from a ceiling, she will do it, only not without multiple sighs and an air of total grievance. (I don't think it's because she's for spider rights.) I should fire her, but I loathe cleaning anything, especially lint in the clothes dryer. She does that without my asking. Almost makes up for her grumpiness.

So now in my home I have fifty-two thousand dollars that don't belong to me. I did indeed count it.

Just the bills on the very top were crisp and new. The ones beneath were obviously used. That's good, right?

That means they can be passed without drawing notice.

The question is am I the owner? It's finders, keepers, wouldn't you say?

Oh, *you're* the owner! Those are your dollars! You left the money behind because you were startled by a raven that landed on the cable car! Or was it that homeless person with TB coughing all over your face? The little ghost boy from 1909 made you drop your satchel?

You know what? I don't believe you.

If I keep the money, am I a thief?

If I report the money to MUNI, will it actually go to the legal owners? What kind of ID do they have?

If nobody claims the satchel, will MUNI find a way to keep the money for itself? Probably. I will be screwed out of it.

If I turn the money in now, won't they say, "Why did you take so long to report it?"

What if it belongs to the Mafia or the Tongs? Will they find out I have it and tear my tongue out with a pair of Tongs? I'd say "He He" except that I am scared shitless that might really happen. There are some MEAN dudes of all races, creeds, and colors out there for whom $52,000 would be very close to their hearts.

What if the Tooth Fairy left it behind for me? I did have a little dental work done on the Saturday before I found it!

Crap! You find a lot of money and then you can't even use it without tearing yourself apart figuring out what to do with it!

∞ ∞

So I left the money on another cable car yesterday. I'm pretty sure nobody saw me. I just couldn't deal with it. Maybe it's being passed from one cable car to the next and eventually will make its way back to me. Hah!

Maybe a drug cartel found its lost money and started to use it as originally intended — to addict grade school kids to studying for their SATs. Now that's a good one.

Hah, hah, hah!

⋆ ⋆

It's been a bad week. I had this recurring dream, more like a nightmare. I realize that other people's dreams are boring, but I need to tell somebody about mine. Please!

I was in this place, let's call it downtown San Francisco. It had lots of tall buildings, hotels and such, department stores, even government buildings and apartments. Some of them were run-down, but many of them looked rather nice, expensive. I kept having this feeling that I wanted to move to this place. I was already living there, but somehow I wanted to move to this place. (You know how contradictory dreams can be.) Yet I had a dream. . .

But something kept holding me back. In fact, there were many things holding me back, people, not really things.

I was walking down the street, then up a hill. My legs were straining, hurting because the hill was so steep.

I knew it was San Francisco because of those hills. All around me were more hills, even steeper ones. I had been winged by a gunshot and could feel my upper torso smarting like hell.

I wasn't naked. I was full dressed in my cable car uniform. I remember feeling lucky that I wasn't naked.

I kept looking down at my brown trousers to make sure I was dressed.

Then I felt people pushing past me. They were not nice. Three of them bumped into me, maybe deliberately, maybe by accident. But they bumped into me, not me into them. I'm sure about that. Still, they got angry and started calling me names. All three of them got right up into my face and snarled at me. I couldn't exactly hear what they were calling me, but it was nasty. They said that if I ever bumped into them again they would kill me. I kept trying to say, "But you bumped into me!" Only the words wouldn't come out.

Yet I had a dream . . .

Then they were gone. For a moment I felt I was safe. Then from across the street two more came towards me, big and threatening. "You hit our friends!" they said together. "No, I didn't!" I answered, or tried to, but no words emerged from my mouth. They wouldn't listen anyway and started hitting me, first with their fists, then with 2x4s. They left splinters in my face and neck. They laughed and called me "a pussy." That word was very distinct.

"You punk pussy!" they kept saying, knocking me down and kicking me in the ribs.

Then two jumped out of a doorway and began robbing me. They yanked my wallet out of my pants pocket, then said, "Is that all you got?" They were outraged that I didn't have more money for them to steal. "You owe us! You owe us, motherfucka!" they said over and over. Strangely, their wrath didn't seem to be about anything I had actually done myself.

Seven more came out of a park on a corner and started hassling me, surrounding me and asking me if I wanted to buy goods from them. I think they meant drugs, but it sounded like "droogs." I kept telling them I didn't want any. They showed me other things from the backs of double-parked cars. They also smashed the windows of other cars as I watched. They pulled packages and stuff from the back seats and the trunks of the cars. "Hey, those aren't your cars!" I told them. "Shut the fuck up, faggot!" they all yelled. "Pay us for these things. "I don't want them. I don't want them!" I cried out. The seven made a circle around me and began threatening me. "You gonna die, sucka!" they chanted. They kept saying it over and over. "I just want to get up this hill!" I insisted. Then they punched me in the mouth. One of them took out a gun and fired it into my ear. For some reason it did not go off. The guy cursed and cracked the gun across my cheek. It hurt like mad, and I told myself, "Wake up! Wake up! Get away!"

But I couldn't wake up. Yeah, I had a dream . . .

Now I lay on the sidewalk bleeding. I had turned into a woman and my skirt was above my knees. Another male came out of the shadows and jumped on top of my body. He had a huge dick and stuck it between my legs. I didn't like it. I hated it! "Get off me!" I screamed. "You want it, bitch!" he said and then he ejaculated and groaned for what seemed forever. "Another one is comin' into you, bitch" he whispered to me. Somehow I managed to roll to the side, mostly because he had been weakened by his ejaculation. "Come back here!" he yelled.

At last I was running down a hill. I wanted to be going up the hill, but I was running down it. So I felt frustrated, glad to have escaped the rapist but unhappy that I couldn't get to my destination. I didn't know what my destination was, only that I *had* to get there!

Then there was guns going off. This time it was men similar to the ones who had said that I had bumped into them. They were shooting in the air, as if to celebrate New Year's or the Fourth of July. Bullets fell down like fireworks, hitting some other men, who grew very angry and started shooting huge guns at the others. Soon everybody was shooting at everybody else. A woman with a stroller was going by with twins in it and was hit by the gunfire. The twins cried and almost fell out of the stroller. Then suddenly they had guns too, even the mother, and were shooting back at the men with these guns. Bodies were falling, with blood spattering everywhere. A big splotch of blood hit my chest. I kept trying and trying to wipe it off, but it wouldn't go away. I had a dream . . .

Then somebody big came up behind me and put his arm across my throat. It was the rapist again. He kept squeezing my throat with his forearm until I thought my eyes would bulge out. I remember thinking, "At least he's not raping me this time!"

Then he tossed me to my knees and started singing to me. His clothes turned all baggy and covered with flashy jewelry. He could not sing at all. His voice was awful. And the words were mostly cuss words and "faggot" this and "punk" that. The rhymes were also terrible, like greeting card verse, only with Murderous Attitude. He threatened to rape me again unless I stayed there and listen to his songs. He forced me to buy a CD of his songs. For some reason, even though I hated his songs, I asked him to sign his autograph on the CD. "It's for Darlene," I said.

It's without question the worst nightmare I have ever had in fifty-two years on this earth. And do you know what the worst part was? There was a name for these horrible, horrible men in my nightmare, but I was not allowed to utter that name. Like in a dark fairy tale, I felt that if I could just utter the name I would be free and the men would stop behaving the way they were, appalled by their own actions if only they could be called what they were. However, a gigantic zipper grew over my mouth, and in my head I kept hearing this loud voice saying, "It is much, much worse to utter this terrible word than to behave like this terrible word! You may not say it. You may not ever say it no matter what they do to you!" My whole body was sweating and I was bursting to shout the word and save myself. But I could not say the word! Oh, I had a dream!

Climbing the hill, climbing and yelling, I finally woke up. Now that I am awake, I still can't remember what that terrible, magical word was that I was unable to utter to save myself. But I think it began with "n."

℃ ℅

I miss Bitty the Second scampering around under my jacket. I don't miss him as much as I thought I would, though. He did not have as much personality as Bitty the First. Rats are just like people. Some have better personalities than others. Only you can choose which pets you want to live with! It's much harder with humans. I suppose.

I could go to some remote island somewhere and live by myself and not get irritated by people. Maybe I'll just do that, after I retire. I have to admit that every once in a while I get a hankering to talk to somebody, anybody. Even you! That's a joke! Can't take a joke? Why did the cable car go up the hill? Answer: Because it was there. Another answer: Because they were put in place before there were automobiles that could climb the hill. Still another answer: Because folks are sentimental about the relics of the past. I'm almost a relic of the past myself, but I doubt anyone is going to be sentimental about Yours Truly. (That's my real name. Did I ever mention it?)

Why did the cable car go down the hill? Because the gripman didn't use the grip properly. (You have been warned.)

I can see the headline now: MAD CABLE DRIVER PLOWS INTO . . . I'll let you fill in the rest. The words "Murder-Suicide" will figure prominently in the story. But will they have it right? "Despondent over Fiancée's Coma." "Angry at the Homeless." "Furious at Tourists." "Raged at the Innocent Undocumented." "Faculties Impaired." "Childless, Bitter, Elderly Rat Fancier." Screw the papers! They always get it wrong. Do you notice the number of retractions they have to print all the time, only they put them in small print way out of sight.

Besides, we use GUNS in my country to kill people, not cable cars! Believe me, I am tempted to get a gun of my own, for real. I used to be against guns, until I got winged by that sniper on top of that building. Now I'm an ex-liberal on that topic. I'm an ex-liberal on a lot of topics, I guess. I'll probably shoot the wrong person if I get shot at again, but at least it will be something! Nothing is worse than feeling totally *helpless*. And even your words are censored!

Which brings me to this woman with her eight kids who rode on my cable car this morning. She was short, bundled up in a long green coat, unsmiling. The kids were ages ten through two, I'd estimate, dressed in hand-me-downs and barefoot. The woman herself looked to be about thirty. So she was still in child-bearing age. I'd didn't see the father or fathers anywhere in sight. Maybe she didn't need a man. She self-populated, like the delicate flowering plant she was. Or maybe God sent the children to her womb miraculously. She was even holier than the Virgin Mary – eight times holier!

I'd be lying if I said the eight kids were misbehaving. They weren't loud, not as loud as the drunks I get all the time now. They sat clustered around their fertile momma as she wiped three runny noses, felt a forehead or two, shook her index finger at the boy with the comic book, and adjusted the youngest one on her lap in umpteen uncomfortable ways. The thought that kept crossing my mind was Why Would Anybody Have Eight Kids?! Sorry, I don't believe for a minute she did it so that her kids' taxes can pay for my Social Security! I saw some other women ooing and awing over the little one. But all I felt was resentment. Was the woman that horny? That religious? That hell-bent on her genes taking over the world? Okay, I have one kid, maybe. This woman had eight! With more to come!

Then two people from one of the Tenderloin "helping" agencies got on board, as they do from time to time. One was this gangly, tall guy with a big, round moon face carrying a clipboard. The other was a woman (or a guy with a bad M to F medical attempt) who had long, flat blonde hair and a lip gloss that called too much attention to her chapped lips. I'd seen the two before. They were after "data" to use for government (city, state, federal, or all of those) "findings" about people in the downtown area. The man plopped himself down on one knee in front of the woman with her brood and asked, "May I ask you some questions about how you have been treated in San Francisco?"

The mother still didn't smile, but she did nod. Immediately the woman, with her clipboard, knelt down next to her agency partner. "Hello, I'm Robyn," she said, shaking the mother's fingertips awkwardly. "We were wondering if you have been the victim of discrimination?" The mother did not reply. Then the male said, "Don't be afraid to tell us. We understand if you feel reluctant to tell us if people have discriminated against you. We are here to help you." He likewise shook the mother's fingertips. The kids sat big-eyed, full of attention. "I am fine," the mother finally said. "We can provide a translator if you cannot understand us," Robyn said. She took a cell phone out of her coat pocket and showed it to the mother.

"We are fine."

"You are entitled to food stamps and family financial assistance," the male said.

"We must get off soon," the mother said, pointing up ahead. The children took that to mean to stand up.

"Hasn't anyone tried to look at your papers, thus violating the law?" Robyn prompted. "They can't do that to you!"

"Even to ask for your driver's license. You don't have to show them anything!"

"Thank you. No." The mother was collecting her brood, making sure that she hadn't missed any.

"Surely, you have been stared at!" Robyn kept going. "Hasn't someone made you feel embarrassed?"

"Why?" the mother said, truly puzzled.

"Because of your beautiful, beautiful children," the male said. He was beginning to sound desperate, about to lose yet another Victim of Discrimination that his agency couldn't save.

I'm sorry, those kids weren't "beautiful, beautiful." They looked thoroughly "ordinary, ordinary."

"Thank you. We are leaving now," the mother said, getting ready for me to stop the cable car.

"Well, whatever you do, don't hesitate to file a complaint with our agency!" Robyn called to the mother and her many offspring as they tumbled their way down to the street. Both Robyn and her partner reached down and forced their agency forms into the hands of the mother and the oldest boy. "You are welcome, so welcome in San Francisco! Our hearts go out to you!"

The mother and brood hurried away like a duck and her ducklings. Robyn and her agency mate gave me a dirty look, suspicious of the look in my eye, I imagine. They conferred and agreed to try other Victims elsewhere and got off at the next stop.

Where do you think the mother with the eight kids was from? Please note: I deliberately did NOT say. Oh, did you assume they were Latin and Catholic? Blacks maybe? Of Mixed Race? Gypsies? No, she and her kids could have been Okies! Or from Marin County! Or Episcopalians! Or Kennedys! How dare you judge them with even a disapproving, discriminatory glance for being so fertile! Maybe you're the rabid, bastard racists, huh?!

My point is that nobody should have eight Victims of any kind! Bay Area schools are overwhelmed with the off-spring of cultures that don't give a shit about the environment or overpopulation as long as they take care of their own personal brood, and yet they are encouraged to think of themselves as Victims! People like me support the over-populators. Hurray for me! Does that make me a Victim? Oh, we're all just human beings in this together? Like hell, we are! It's a competition, and I'm losing!

03 80

A funny thing happened on the way to the cable car this morning. A man on a street corner was selling a pamphlet called "Your Inner Peace of Mind." Naturally I stopped to peruse the goods. Who doesn't want inner peace of mind? I'd even take some outer peace of mind.

"Good morning, sir," the pamphlet man said. He was quite short, wearing a respectable brown suit from one of the men's warehouses, prominent ears on both sides, oozing warmth and good will toward mankind.

"How much is it?" I enquired.

"We will worry about that later, sir. For now, I just want you to take the first step to a whole new life."

I flipped through the pamphlet. There were chapters on "Finding Your Hidden Potential," "The First Small Step Onto the Real Path of Your Life," and "Happiness Is Yours for the Taking." Sounded good to me! "I'll take one," I said. "How much?"

"No, sir, the price is immaterial. It is more than just the price of my pamphlet."

I was running late to work now and needed to be going, but somehow I knew I couldn't keep being angry all the time. "Let us begin with one item that you would like to change in your life."

"There are so many," I confessed.

"You are not alone, sir." The short man touched my elbow in a comforting way. "We have all been there."

I couldn't move, entranced by the man's soothing words, as he began to spell out the principles of his group's philosophy. "We support a system that sees the world as the Kind and the Unkind. May I ask what kind you are, sir?"

"I guess I'm pretty Unkind," I admitted.

"You can let go of the negativity. It is possible!" The man's lips all but trembled with calm resolution.

"But how will I recognize myself then?!" I joked, sort of.

"We do not try to change the core of any person. We just round off the edges of the troubled chi."

"Did you say chi or cheese?"

"I enjoy your wit, sir." He laughed a little fake laugh for my sake. "I used to be like you, brittle of word, judgmental of heart."

"But then you got a pamphlet, is that it? And you changed?"

"You will get your pamphlet, sir. I assure you."

Next I expected to hear about his once-a-month pamphlet plan, available this week only, and discounted just for me as a new customer. However, he didn't say that. He said, "I want you to wear this button. It is completely free. I guarantee that if you wear this button for two days you will feel your whole life begin to change. In time, you will transform from the Unkind to the Kind."

"Just from wearing this button?" I asked.

"Oh, it is not quite that easy, sir. It is just the first phase. I will be here on this street corner or the next for the coming week. Wear the button and when you see me next, tell me how you have altered. I guarantee you that you will have begun to feel your very soul in its migration to the better, happier you."

"But what if I don't see you around?"

"Oh, you will see me, sir. It is to be. Of that I am sure."

He held out the button. I took it. And then he left without giving me the pamphlet.

Yes, I read what was on the button. BE, it said. Okay. Why not? I thought.

I wore the damn button for three whole days and then I threw it into a gutter. I never saw the button man again. I'm sorry a button is not enough. I don't like shorthands and I don't like pornography, even when it's spiritual.

So I remain a crabby Old Fart. Yay me.

The really funny part is that I have changed of late.

I was quite the little mushy liberal, safe in my lower-middle-class white cocoon, back before Stockton became a nightmare of foreclosures and crime. I felt so morally superior to my parents. Now I am becoming my parents, probably even less accepting than they were. The really troublesome part is that I have changed because of what I have seen, heard, and endured IN MY FACE on the cable cars of San Francisco. I'm not studying sociological graphs and dry analyses of demographics. I AM LIVING THEM!

I completely understand why people go berserk in this country. I am close to that myself. And I am getting a gun now for sure, I think: Okay, it won't cure all the problems, and some of the wrong people will get wasted along with the guilty ones, and most likely I'll be killed too, but what the Hell? It will be a start. Maybe it will even bring to a halt the transformation of the world of the cable car in downtown San Francisco, from the charming, old-timey "San Francisco treat," into the cesspool that is climbing over my shoes up to my knees each day I go to work. Old farts aren't always wrong, you know.

I wish I could leave my job – so that I could be liberal again.

CB EO

Aside from the hundreds of other things that have been building and building the last few months, today it was the offer of a bribe. Tips I can live with – not that there are many of those from my passengers. They assume I get paid well by MUNI. With overtime, I do. So a thank you (rarer and rarer, by the way) for my driving them up or down a hill or two is perfectly acceptable. I don't even need a thank you. The omission of a slap to the back of my head or one less gob of nose phlegm blown onto where I sit, or even not stealing my identity, is all I ask, I swear! But when this young buck from South America or Central America or one of those islands in the sun jumps ahead in line to board my cable car and orders me to take off immediately, leaving the rest of the boarding passengers behind, I take umbrage. He pulls out a fifty dollar bill, probably counterfeit, and snaps it close to my face. "You like?" he says. "*Vamanos!*" Not only did he violate my personal space, he violated my sense of

Who the Fuck Do You Think You Are! He seemed to believe that he could buy me for fifty bucks. I said, "Sit down, hombre! You're out of line." Then he called me a "*puta*." (When all else fails, call somebody a *puta*!)

"You think you can buy me for *fifty* bucks?!" I literally screamed. "How dare you? How dare you?"

And, no, I was not for sale for *sixty* bucks, either. Fuck you.

ෆ ෨

Now for a hundred bucks? Well, maybe we could talk.

I'm kidding. I'm kidding.

You have to kid or you go berserk.

Maybe you go berserk even if you kid?

ෆ ෨

I'm getting afraid of myself. I think I'm may be having a breakdown of some kind. It may take just one more straw to break this camel's back. I learned today from her doctor that Darlene has taken a turn for the worse, and he doesn't think she's going to come out of her coma. Ever. He predicts that she will just fade until she fades out. For God's sake, she's only 58 years old! That's it? You just struggle and struggle and then you die? Somebody just turns off your machine? This can't be right. It can't be.

And then I had to fill in for Sam What's His Name today on the cable car. Not his real name. It's long and unspellable. He was out with some communicable disease. (I think his daughter was also having triplets!) I was looking forward to a day off, but, no, I filled in.

And guess who gets on my cable car early this morning around 10? This black teenager, with his butt hanging over his pants tops, a flashy jacket with umpteen sports insignia all over it, his cap turned sideways, and topped with the unfriendliest face a teenager can put on a human skull. Not only was he not giving up his seat to whitey, he was taking up three seats so that nobody else could sit down. Of course his name WASN'T Darnell or anything close – how could it possibly be?! And of course he was filling out his application for a Rhodes Scholarship as he spread out his legs as wide as possible. Yeah, right. You watch too many phony TV shows. I live in the real world!

When he got up, he accidentally bumped into this tall Chinese dude carrying a basketful of live baby turtles. I am not making this up! Instead of apologizing, the black teenager gets all huffy and bent out of shape. If you haven't seen the type, what rock have you been living under? He then starts harassing the guy with the baby turtles, who refuses to apologize. He had no reason to apologize. The black guy had bumped into him! I saw the whole thing with my own eyes. I couldn't make out every word that ensued, but "disrespected me" and "honky, chink ass" came up more than once. The tall Chinese guy stood there stoically, no doubt hoping it would all come to a stop and blow away. Only non-Darnell wasn't having it. His voice kept getting louder and louder, and my conductor was no help. Before you could say, "I have a dream," the Rhodes Scholar pulls out a handgun and threatens the Chinese turtle guy. He went all Rap Badass and tried to pistol whip the man he had bumped into. The Chinese guy even offered his basket of baby turtles to the black teen, as some kind of appeasement. He was refused. "We're not taking your shit no more!" the offended party (also the offending party) spat.

"Hey!" I half-yelled. Any more than that and I thought I might get shot.

What happened? The black teenager shot the Chinese guy, spilling all the baby turtles (his lunch somewhere?) on the floor of the cable car. In fact, he shot him twice. He tried a third time, but his handgun jammed. (I guess they just don't make those Saturday Night Specials like they used to! Made with shoddy workmanship and extra lead in China?)

People did rush to help the guy who had fallen. He was saved from bleeding to death by a passenger. (Who applied acupuncture needles to the wounds!. . . No, Western medicine reared its ugly head and took over, imperialistic as usual.) They even helped gather up his baby turtles and whisked him off to a hospital in Chinatown, I presume.

The black thug waited around for a while, looking a little worried, but mostly smug and self-righteous, holding his handgun for us to see, all snotty and gangsta, like it was an extra penis. Then he jumped off the moving cable car and disappeared into the crowd. I thought when integration came, it was supposed to lift up the oppressed. It seems more like it has turned the oppressed into the oppressors. Over the years it has gone from you're bad just because you're black, to you can't be blamed for any shit you do, because you're black!

Don't you envy me my Public Sector job? You may not like me or my opinions, but at least they're *my* opinions and I earned them the hard way.

ෆ ෂ

Why do I keep insisting on talking about race and ethnicity? It probably makes you uncomfortable. It makes me uncomfortable. But I keep harping on it, because I am constantly told I cannot. I am only free to kiss ass, and I don't like ass. Plenty of whites are criminals and assholes too, but I see the other groups leading the way statistically, and most people are so goddamned P.C., the truth can't get out! So crime increases day by day, and not only can't you do anything about it, as they say about the weather, you can't even talk about it except under your breath! Dear old quaint San Francisco therefore is being mugged, mucked-up, and murdered before my very eyes. No Yay!

I have a solution, or a partial one. People are all wrong about never using the word "nigger." The opposite should be true. We should use it to describe ugly, low-life behavior wherever it occurs. Maybe it'll help stop it. "That's very nigger of you." "Stop being a nigger." Needless to say, it could apply to any culprit, no matter what color.

☙ ❧

Carlos Molina does repairs for MUNI. He is not a bad guy, or wasn't until what happened happened. He's good with tools. He is about forty, more South American Indian than Spanish in his DNA, I'd venture. (Can you venture someone's DNA any longer?) I know that you not permitted to use "retarded" nowadays. That's 'offensive.' Even when describing this fucking imbecile who steals transfers on the cars and sells them. He looks like he has Down's syndrome, but he's pretty quick with the stealing. So maybe "retarded" is the wrong word, after all. Down's syndrome is the new Einstein.

As to Carlos, no, he is not retarded in the slightest. He is a roly-poly, big-chested fellow, a bit bowlegged. He wears work boots and usually has a leather tool belt around his waist. He used to complain that his waist was getting too thick for his belt, so he punched some extra holes in it with an awl, if that's what it's called.

So why am I telling you about Carlos? Because he Went Bad, that's why. He got greedy. He was making a very good salary doing MUNI repairs. There had been a few rumors that maybe Carlos and some of his pals had actually damaged some MUNI property, electricity poles on buses, streetcar tracks, and such, in order to 'help' business. I didn't believe that, believe it or not, just chalked it up to rumor. Carlos Molina was always nice to me.

So why mention Carlos's last name? Because it is completely relevant to what he did. Because I'm not supposed to!

Yesterday he was caught red-handed in a sting that MUNI had set up. He was just one of a bunch of men with ties to gangs in the Mission, to whom he has been selling genuine parts and substituting inferior, unsafe parts in return. MUNI caught on to the scam some time ago and traced the bad parts switch all the way up to some top officials. But MUNI didn't expose them for fear of being "culturally insensitive." The corrupt officials, you must understand, claimed that they did not know that taking bribes, dealing in cracked and crummy unsafe parts, having business dealings with gangs, and putting their profiteering over the financial well-being and downright safety of the people riding MUNI were wrong. "Everybody does it back home!" they claimed, or words to that effect. Carlos Molina and the others have not been fired, just transferred. And MUNI had to apologize for its "insensitivity" when there were several large demonstrations in the Mission. Yeah, yeah, an Amendment of the US Constitution says you can't say boo about people because of the country of their origin, but COME ON!!! You don't have to let them kill you with their customs!

The hoopla made me check out my cable car. Don't usually get down and check the two-foot-long wooden track brakes myself. Today I did. Sure enough, the Monterey Fir had been replaced with crummier wood. It was already worn through. The whole brake system there was metaphorically hanging by a thread, a two-foot-wide thread, but a thread nonetheless. A lot of people could have been killed. We can't have that. (Or can we? Might shake things up.)

C)3 8)

The cable cars used to be just an occasional target in the overall crime statistics. Now it seems we're being sought out for special attention. We are So Quaint and Picturesque, you see.

A few days had barely gone by after the handgun and turtles incident on my cable car when another crazy person did His Thing in my presence. This one was a WHITE ex-Marine (named G.I. Joe, no doubt. I did not learn his actual name until it wound up in the

Chronicle.) See, it's the content of his character I want to bitch about!

Apparently, he was having post-something-something syndrome. (Thanks, George W. Bush and Dick Head Cheney and your dumb-ass wars!) He had skinned a neighbor's cat in one of the suburbs in the East Bay, beaten his wife and her cousin to death in the cousin's garage, and tried to shoot a cop with an AR-15 he had brought back from the front. All this was before he got to my cable car. He should have known you can skin a cat in Milpitas, but God help you if you target a cop!

So I was dealing with a dead man walking – I mean, a dead man pulling an assault weapon out of what looked like a cloth carrying case. I'm not good at naming the types of assault weapons. Does the type really matter? G.I. Joe had altered it anyway from its original form so that he could load more ammunition into it. The Second Amendment told him he had to!

He stood on a couple of seats at the back of my cable car as I headed up Powell Street for what must have been my three thousandth time, or more, and he starts shooting at random. At random!!! You bet your ass! It wasn't as loud as I thought it would be. Did he have a silencer on the weapon? Can you put a silencer on an assault weapon – so that you won't possibly deafen anybody you're shooting!?

I was so stunned, even with all the crap that had been happening in the last year on the cable car, that I didn't apply the brakes. I also am not as strong since I got shot. Maybe I could have jolted the ex-Marine over the rear of the cable car – and then backed the cable car over the white bastard. I just kept driving up the hill. My conductor, Leonard Longfeather, began to ring his conductor's bell and tussle with the shooter, but he was no match for the ex-Marine and was knocked to his knees and then kicked in the head (had his bell rung, you might say) and was out flat on his back before you could say "Geronimo!" (Lenny Longfeather always claimed that he was half Cherokee, but I think he made that up. Maybe a little Native American, way back.) They really played up his "native" roots in the media coverage, though.

The ex-Marine made it up as far as Sacramento Street before the cops got him. About twelve San Francisco police cars, plus at least two from Milpitas, and one Highway Patrol descended on that sucker every which way from Sunday. (Is that even English? I'm started to forget! Zing!) He was wearing a bullet-proof vest, the papers said.

I didn't see any bullet-proof vest. Whatever he was wearing didn't matter. It wasn't going to stop that cascade of bullets flying through the air. G.I. Joe fell straight down off the back of the cable car, head first, getting off a volley as he fell.

OMG, it was better than a video game!

There was no reset button on this one, however.

A cop from San Francisco lost an ear. A tourist from Luxembourg lost a tooth. Two sheriffs from Milpitas lost their lives, one right there, the other three days later. Wasn't much of G.I. Joe to clean up. But they did. Much was made of the fact that the villain was *white*.

I bet if I'd had my own gun I would have got that guy. (Or he, me.)

ᘓ ᘔ

I started out with this memoir about my Fabulous Cable Car Days, but it seems to be turning into a Manifesto. Does it sound like a MANIFESTO to you? Aren't those always described as "rambling"? Am I rambling? I think I sound pretty coherent, if upset and angry. Is this a tale of why people shouldn't have guns???!!! (That's a joke, son. Are you laughing? Do I have to put LOL or LMAO to point out the wonderful humor of it all? How many exclamation points turn it into a MANIFESTO!!!!!!??????

C8 80

Nothing bad happened on the cable cars today! Hurray! Is that the end of this book then? That's it? It just stops here? Like life?

No, I have a new job. I will sit on a raised platform at the rear of a new cable car, where I will tell sweet, sentimental tales (carefully picked by MUNI and the Board of Supervisors). I will be a tremendous, beloved hit, like all those animal vet tales set in Yorkshire back when!

So come see me on the cable cars! I'll tell you a story to make your heart leap with joy! Less dirty than the Canterbury Tales! More magical than The Arabian Nights! More wholesome than a Disney movie! My little ghost boy son looked me up, and now we are best friends. (People will love it and make me rich!)

C8 80

Oh, wait.

Today's events more than made up for yesterday's quiet time. Some homeless men and women, filthy in clothing and language, of Blended Unknown Races and Colors and Creeds – it goes without saying! – got on my car today and seemed to have lost any charm they may have had back Once Upon a Time. Like ten years ago maybe.

They didn't pay, naturally. They have learned that we can't or won't force them to. They have stopped being the Downtrodden Poor and have become the Total Sons-of-Bitches. They bum cigarettes from passengers, light up, throw the lighted butts on the floor. They carry bottles of cheap booze and guzzle away openly. One guy was shooting up. They aren't so much "homeless" as drunks, drug addicts, and the mentally ill. I used to feel sorry for them and even gave them handouts. Not anymore. Okay, I feel a little sympathy for the woman who sat there scratching her exposed boobs with her fingertips and singing "One Day More" from *Les Miz*. Okay, it wasn't from *Les Miz*. It was some song I didn't recognize because it came from inside the woman's poor, addled head. (It might have been some form of "I'm Looking Over a Four-Leaf Clover.")

When Sabina, my lady conductor of the day, spoke to them nicely and asked them to keep it down or else get off the cable car, they started calling her names. "Goddamned, dick-licking yuppy bitch!" was one of the sweeter ones. "You gentrified cunt!" was another.

A businessman in his fifties in a very expensive-looking grey suit tried to keep reading his stock portfolio or whatever it was and ignore the "homeless," but he wasn't having much luck. He is from the heart of the Financial District and loves to ride the cable cars even though it means he has to walk over a few blocks. "It keeps me trim," he's told me any number of times. "All the better to hedge your funds!" I say back. He thinks I'm funny. (Actually I suspect that he and his ilk are responsible for lots of ruined pensions, foreclosures, and a big dip in the value of the few IRA funds I've managed to accumulate by age 52. So screw him too and the money train he rode in on! Hey, see! I'm an equal-opportunity hater!)

The "homeless" folks spotted Mr. Hedge Fund and started giving him a hard time. Hey, as long as it wasn't me!

"You want some of my ass?" an elderly gentlewoman of no teeth, brown gums, and terminal dirty-bathtub breath asked him. She tried lifting her skirts, but there were so many of them she couldn't quite manage. "For you, a hundred bucks," she added.

At first Mr. Hedge Fund did not respond, then something seemed to flicker in his eye as I checked on him. "Surely that ass is worth at least two hundred," he said.

"Three hundred!" Brown Gums said. Up went two skirts to her knees.

"Not a penny less than five hundred smackeroos for you, Madame."

Now the other "homeless" joined in, taunting Mr. Hedge Fund about his stinginess and his wealth, whooping it up and topping one another with higher and higher offers. In case, I didn't make it clear. These were offers for this old broad's well-caked, hemorrhoidal asshole. (To tell the truth, I think both parties weren't just joking!) I finally had to break it up when an irate mother with her thirteen-year-old daughter confronted me. "Can't you *do* something?!" she demanded, seething with quiet outrage. "I have my daughter with me!"

"Think of them as colorful characters in an exotic land – like New York City!" I offered. (I really think she was worried because her daughter was taking pictures with a cell phone and learning the going price of selling her ass in Merrie Olde San Francisco.)

Yeah, the whole thing was pretty gross.

CB BO

This afternoon some school kids from several public schools as well as a Christian school and a Catholic school got on my car, as they do more often than I like. Usually their parents must pick them up or they have drivers' licenses. For some reason they were having an outing today. It was a nice day for an outing. It was about seventy, fog-less, no nip in the air, bright but not overly so. San Francisco can be chilly much of the time. This is not California! It's San Francisco.

I don't know what's happened to American kids over the past forty-some years, but it's not good. And I don't say that as just an old crank. Others have noticed it too. Tests scores have documented it as well. I've beheld it face to face, on many an afternoon. How shall I phrase it? They are BRATS. From early on they are told they are special, marvelous, future presidents of the United States of America, all without the faintest shred of evidence. It's one thing to be good to your kids. It's quite another to tell them lies about their Enormous Value. They are so mouthy and full of themselves it almost defies description. Not only do they believe that their poop does not stink, they believe that other people love their poop and can't wait to see it in the toilets they don't ever flush. If they behave in class the way do on the cable cars, and I've heard they do, don't blame the teachers for the schools! Blame the brats for acting like brats!

Some of them were rough-housing on my cable car this afternoon. We were up at the turn-around at Maritime Park. You cannot have a more beautiful vista than that spot. The blue Pacific Ocean, the Golden Gate Bridge, sailboats and the occasional passing freighter – it's spectacular. And yet I feel the need to gripe. I have become the "gripeman," alas. I don't even want to hear myself anymore. But, hey, maybe somebody with power will read this memoir and do something about the deteriorating world of the cable cars, my world. Please, I beg you!

When I say "rough-housing," I don't mean the sort of horseplay and teasing of my own high school days back in Stockton. I was taunted and even punched a few times. I taunted and punched a few guys myself. I even had a fistfight with a girl once. Her name was Big Sally and she beat the shit out of me! But in my defense, she did have a ring on when she fought me. I guess I should have been grateful she wasn't carrying a pistol. (The scar that ring made on my lower throat remains to this day, although somewhat faded. The gradually crinkling skin there almost covers it now! Let's hear it for old age!)

These kids today on my cable car are a whole different breed. Did I really just write "these kids today"?! I swore that I would never utter such words. It's the kind of thing my father was always saying. "These kids today are listening to that rocky roll!" That's what he called it: "rocky roll." These kids today don't seem to know the difference between 'like' and 'as.'" Sure, Dad, you were right on that one! It was the beginning of the fall of civilization. Rest assured that they make up for any missing grammar with the word "like" by using it UMPTEEN TIMES in every single sentence.

If only we could get back to the Age of Innocence, with mere fistfights and minor lapses in usage! "These days" I'm talking about really unpleasant antics, pretty much every time kids ride the cable cars. They even get to ride for free instead of having to pay or use a Fast Pass. Still, it doesn't make them grateful. It doesn't even make them civilized. They make the Visigoths seem like Avon ladies. Know-It-All Know Nothings.

For instance, one "kid," taller than me, and I'm six foot tall, snatched some girl's knitted cap off her head and sailed it over the hill at Maritime Park, laughing like a hyena. I guess he thought he was "courting," the way certain kinds of inarticulate boys always have. In this case he couldn't retrieve the cap, nor could the girl, and she was out a perfectly good article of wearing apparel. She was so pissed off, that boy is never going to get into her pants, never in a million years, no matter what he thought his little trick was going to accomplish. In fact, she picked up a large stick and cracked it over his head – hard, not girlie. Everybody got all excited and even noisier, hormones of all types flying hither and thither. I am supposed to report such incidents on the cars, but if I did, I'd be filling out reports ALL the time.

Instead, I warned the cap tosser and the stick wielder, and of course both of them turned on me. "It's none of your fucking business!" the tall tosser informed me. "She's my girlfriend!"

"You destroy the property of your girlfriend?" I said incredulously.

"Like hell, he's my boyfriend!" the girl protested. "He's a shit sandwich!"

I'm so out of it now I couldn't tell if "shit sandwich" might be some form of endearment. I've heard people use "sick" that way. "That's positively sick!" said with reverence in the voice. I can't keep up with the latest slang. I don't even try anymore. Slang dies faster than sperm anyway.

The kids weren't especially going anywhere today, it seemed to me, just milling around at the park's turn-around. They couldn't seem to agree on whether to stay there or ride back to the other end at Market Street. I thought the incident was over, when suddenly one other kid, a fat, small one in a Catholic school sweatshirt, started screaming. He held up his hand. There was a rat trap hanging from his thumb. Two girls in similar outfits, only girl versions, the skirt part surprisingly short, were bent over with hysterical amusement. Evidently they had somehow tricked Fat Boy into putting his thumb in a rat trap. "You said it wouldn't hurt! You said it wouldn't hurt!" Fat Boy kept yelling in this sissy-boy voice. The other kids were congratulating the two Catholic school girls on their success in "getting" Fat Boy. Maybe Fat Boy was a mean prick himself, but a rat trap on his thumb, with full snap? What if he had had it snapped off? Somehow I got the feeling that would have made the others laugh even harder.

I shook my head. (And a lot of good that did!) I jumped back on the cable car and signaled to some straggling passengers to hurry and get aboard if they wanted a ride. That's when the piece de resistance occurred, at least for today. I am positive that not a one of the kids had so much as stolen a glance at the beautiful ocean or the bridge. They had no doubt seen it all too many times already. But they did have time to sass me when I said I was leaving. "You serve the public, loser!" this little punk tells me, arms akimbo.

"What the fuck?!" I said.

He was joined by several more. "You can't order us around!" one of them said.

"We'll leave when we tell you to leave!" came another voice from the Nasty Bunch.

"Fuck the whole fucking lot of you!" I yelled as I released the brake and headed away from the turn-around, leaving the underage assholes behind.

Guess what! They reported me to MUNI and I got a formal reprimand. There is now a Formal Reprimand in my employee file. I was "rude to the public," the report says. "Showed disrespect." Rude? Disrespectful? They're lucky I didn't shoot them. I keep my gun with me now, right where Bitty the First and Bitty the Second used to take their naps, in my armpit. No, I'm not allowed to have it. But I don't feel safe without it. If I see those brats again and they say one word to me, I may shut their goddamned, stupid, snotty mouths forever. We'll see who the "disrespectful, rude losers" are, won't we?

Is there nobody nice left in the world? Not even kids? They are the future, right? Not even Christian kids? What kind of future will that be? So I support this idea of teachers having guns in the schools, not to protect the students from mass shootings – to protect themselves from the students!

È »

It has been months since I last wrote in this Manifesto, journal, memoir, whatever the hell this is. If there are more typos than usual, please excuse them. You'll understand in a bit.

It has truly come at last. Let's call it the FINAL final straw. It came near the end of my shift around five that day, two months ago, as it was getting dark because of daylight savings time. A large man with a megaphone boarded the cable car. "We're about to change staff," I told the guy, in my most public-pleasing voice. I knew I was on probation with MUNI.

"I have a message to deliver!" the large man replied. He was about 6'4" if he was an inch, dressed in a suit that had seen better days, stained with various dropped meals over the previous decade, probably never dry cleaned. He was wearing a minister's collar, which could have been home-made. At least it didn't seem to fit right. He had a very large Adam's apple and some stubble on the lower half of his bony face, and I am sorry to report that he was white. He put the megaphone up to his lips and began addressing the area around the cable car, even though nobody was there except me. "The Apocalypse is coming!" said he.

"You tell it, my brother," I said, ironically and under my breath.

His eye caught mine. "The answer is Jesus Christ!" he shouted into the megaphone, causing it to distort.

"That's Jesus H. Christ!" I agreed, sort of.

"The righteous shall be saved in His bosom. The guilty and the damned shall perish in the everlasting flames of Hellfire!"

"Sounds right to me," I said. I shook my hands in the air on either side of my head to show that I was feeling the Spirit. "Or when the cable car crashes at the bottom of the hill and all shall perish, not just the Bad."

"The wicked and fallen shall feed the gnashing teeth of Beelzebub's minions!"

"The metaphor is a little mixed, but I get your message, my brother," I led him on.

He seemed excited that he had a follower. I'm sure the poor guy went around all the time shouting into his megaphone, or the wind, and people fled from his presence. They had their lives to live, their sins to commit! Hallelujah!

"The Lord will divide the blessed from the wicked and put the holy on His right hand, while the unholy will cry out in their hopelessness for all eternity!"

It seemed a little excessive for getting a blow job while your girlfriend was in a coma, but who said the world was fair? So why not the Afterlife as well? "You tell it and sell it, my friend!" I encouraged him. "But will the world listen and repent?!" he asked – rhetorically, I think. "Not on their lives! They continue to displease their God with all manner of fleshly and godless and evil wickedness!" His megaphone was growing more and more distorted, but he didn't seem to notice or care. "Yet God Almighty is not mocked! He sees into every heart and knows what lies there. Your words will not satisfy Him, your prayers will not appease Him, nothing you do will save you from the final annihilation if there is insincerity inside your heart! Do you hear me?" He shook the megaphone. "God is speaking to you through me! And, lo, he shall lay waste to the depraved and the disobedient, to any and all who refuse his Infinite Mercy!"

I wanted to clean up the trash from the day's shift and so I said, as I moved up onto a cable car step and held onto a pole: "You are preaching to the *converted*, pal. Yet the day is done for now. Amen!" The irony of this crackpot and I being on the same general wave length did not escape me.

All of a sudden Holy Man registers something on his stubbly face. His eyes fell on mine in a very personal way, as if a shadow had passed over him. He now realized that I was not a devotee, however much he sort of reminded me very much of myself. He sensed for the first time that I was just mocking him and therefore Mocking God too. "Come here, you!" he said to me, holding the megaphone high above his head.

Then I lost it, totally lost it. "Who the fuck do you think you are?!" I screamed. "Get the fuck off my cable car before I kill you! You and your Devil's spawn! All of you! All of you! Go away and die! Die! Die, you fucking shit heads!" I screamed so hard and so long my head felt like it was about to burst. I jumped up and down and screamed until my voice turned into a rasp and hurt my throat.

Holy Man was for a moment surprised by the screaming, crazy MUNI man. But as sure as I knew anything, I knew that he was going to bash my head in with that megaphone. He started moving toward me, flushed in the face, lumbering. I managed to let go of the pole and jumped down to the street, tweaking my ankle, and started backing up, my hands held up in front of me. But I was not moving fast enough. Damn those tired old legs! Holy Man took something out of his inner suit jacket pocket and aimed it at me. It looked like a Mace canister. Before I could escape, he started spraying the contents at me. He got me good – first on the palms of my hands, then on my chest, then directly on my face, then finally in my eyes. It wasn't Mace. "He who will not see shall be blind!" he cried out. It was some form of sulfuric acid that he had let loose.

CB BO

It's been several months since what happened in the section above occurred, and this is the first time since I have had a chance to write about it in this "Manifesto," journal, memoir, last will and testament, whatever. Do you need a witness for a last will? I can't see any longer. Not since the acid attack by Holy Man on what turned out to be my last day of work. He got my eyes. Even some in my mouth. I can still talk a little, but I sound raspy and can't get much out without coughing. I'm on Disability. It's something.

Darlene passed away a month ago. At least she didn't have to see my burned eyes. Or my burnt-out heart. How's this for a title for this book? "I Left My Burnt-Out Heart in San Francisco"?! They say she's in a Better Place. The Holy Man was declared a loony and moved into a home for the criminally insane. I think it's in Better Place, Utah, a federal facility. He'd probably go to Hell, if there was one.

I just licked some honey and peanut butter off a plate that I made for my lunch. Absolutely delicious. I think I had begun to take peanut butter and honey on an English muffin for granted. . . Still, it's not enough.

It's not working out, and I am signing off. At first I thought I would use the gun I bought not that long ago at the gun show at the Cow Palace. But since I can't see now, I was afraid I might do a really messy job of it. Darlene sometimes had trouble sleeping and kept some pills around my place. It wasn't easy to find them, but I did. I was quite determined.

No, I haven't talked to anybody, except you. How sad is that!? I'm tired of going to Kaiser for "rehabilitation" and "physical therapy" for my hands and earning to walk again, this time without being able to see. There is a mobile van that picks me up.

I did manage to find the little ghost boy, not the one on the cable cars, the one that I sired with the

American Indian blind woman. I tracked him down, found that his mother had died and he had been living with a foster family even before she did. I met with him once, through the family's graciousness. He was a bit wary, but I did give him a hug and a kiss on the top of his head. We both cried, no doubt for different reasons, him probably for having had a blind mother and now a blind father! I am also leaving him my condo, which is again increasing in value, and any other money I have. He should have some money that way and not be so bitter and not have to push anybody off the cable cars! Now also he has at least *one* memory of his phantom father, as I do of my phantom child.

But it's <u>not</u> <u>enough</u>. Just isn't.

I'm between a rock and a hard place. I can't see any longer, and I don't like what I might see. You cannot talk honestly about most things in San Francisco. People keep referring to the bad old attitudes, as if I'm in a box from the past. However, I am talking about what I see NOW. If I am guilty of "racism," then I embrace my "racism." Am I crazy or is the world?

So goodbye. Have a hearty. May your life be a grand one. At least you won't have to hear the goddamned cable car guy bitching anymore!

Still, I am hopeful that if anybody finds this book, they will clean up the typos, not "clean it up" in other ways, and put it up on Amazon.com. I guess, for what it's worth, it's my legacy.

Oh, and here's a cure for a jaundiced view of things: take two aspirins, a scenic ride on a cable car, and bathe the eyes in sulfuric acid. Works every time.

CB ꙮ

OFFICIAL OBITUARY
FOR DEVIN "CORKY" CORCORAN

We here at MUNI in the Cable Car Division are very sorry to report that one of our colleagues, Devin ("Corky") Corcoran, has passed away at the age of fifty-three.

A Stockton native and long-time resident of San Francisco, Mr. Corcoran devoted over nearly thirty years of his life to the service of our company and his beloved city.

Mr. Corcoran, or "Corky" as he loved to be known, will be missed by all, staff and customers alike. He was a talented and faithful gripman on the three lines of our famous cable cars. He was known for his cheery disposition and his expert bell ringing and his welcoming smile.

He will be interred at the Columbarium on Lorraine Court in the city's Richmond District. A non-denomination service is being scheduled. A notice will be issued when the details become fully known.

"Corky" will be laid to rest in his own niche at the Columbarium alongside his beloved fiancée, Darlene Dupree, who preceded him in death.

Donations in either name can be made with the Columbarium.

It has come to light that "Corky" was working on his memoirs when he unexpectedly became a victim of a troubled passenger and suffered severe injuries from which he failed to recover. His memoirs, which were unfinished, are reported by those who have read them to be a delightful, gracious, and warm font of happy memories of his time as "Corky the Cheery Gripman" on the City's fabled cable cars. They will be buried with him, in accordance with Mr. Corcoran's wishes.

Although we mourn his passing, we are pleased that our favorite gripman was able to serve out his working days on his beloved cable cars, as they made their way "halfway to the stars." "Corky," our dear buddy, we are sure that you are all the way to the stars by now!

Further, we know that you would be heartbroken to learn, as the rest of us have, that there has been a recent, unfortunate development at MUNI. Due to budget cuts, equipment problems, a few accidents, some on-going legal expenses, changing consumer needs, and a general call for more modernization in the City by the Bay's transportation system, the last three remaining cable car lines will be shut down permanently at the end of this year.

Yes, it is the end of an era. But we are sure that the San Francisco's Future holds even more promise than San Francisco's fabulous, bygone, legendary past! We know that "Corky" would be proud!

ß ∂